TWO COULD PLAY AT THE SAME DANGEROUS GAME

Sarah did not have to be privy to the secrets and scandals of society to clearly see that there was more between her husband and his beautiful cousin Annabella than he wanted her to know.

It was very easy for Sarah to suspect that the love that had bound Lord Peter Marchman to her in distant America had suffered a sea change when transported to aristocratic London.

It was even easier to listen to the handsome, elegant, irresistibly charming Gervais Fallon when that accomplished rake suggested she repay her husband's indiscretions in kind.

Taking revenge by yielding to temptation—the combination seemed sinfully sweet....

MARCHMAN'S LADY

MARCHMAN'S LADY

by

Caroline Brooks

A SIGNET BOOK

NEW AMERICAN LIBRARY

NAL BOOKS ARE AVAILABLE AT QUANTITY DISCOUNTS
WHEN USED TO PROMOTE PRODUCTS OR SERVICES.
FOR INFORMATION PLEASE WRITE TO PREMIUM MARKETING DIVISION,
NEW AMERICAN LIBRARY, 1633 BROADWAY,
NEW YORK, NEW YORK 10019.

SIGNET TRADEMARK REG. U.S. PAT. OFF. AND FOREIGN COUNTRIES
REGISTERED TRADEMARK—MARCA REGISTRADA
HECHO EN CHICAGO, U.S.A.

SIGNET, SIGNET CLASSIC, MENTOR, PLUME,
MERIDIAN AND NAL BOOKS
are published by New American Library,
1633 Broadway, New York, New York 10019

First Printing, February, 1986

1   2   3   4   5   6   7   8   9

PRINTED IN THE UNITED STATES OF AMERICA

Part One

Santimoke, Maryland
August 1814

1

Water Garden, that old and charming estate of the Goldsborough family, was known far and wide for the charm and quality of its hospitality. Not even war could dim the party that Col. George Goldsborough and his good lady, known to one and all as Miss Henrietta, gave in honor of their only daughter's nineteenth birthday. When, after four sons, Miss Henrietta had presented her colonel with a baby girl, there had been great cause for rejoicing at Water Garden, and it seemed only right and proper to them that this event should be annually celebrated with a great ceremony and celebration.

In spite of the fact that a British blockade ship had stood off the Santimoke River, at the foot of their sweeping lawns, for more than a fortnight, the celebration continued undeterred, and Water Garden, blazing with lights, was filled with all of the gentry of the Eastern Shore, most of whom were connected to the Goldsboroughs by blood or marriage.

Few people turned down an invitation to a party at Water Garden, for it was well known that the punch bowls would be filled to overflowing, the feast laid out upon the long Sheraton table in the dining room bountiful, the card tables set up in the study and the billiard table in the orangerie ready for play, and the dancing in the ballroom to continue into the dawn.

Even though Water Garden had eight bedrooms, there would be many a young man who would sleep on a shakedown in the library or the veranda this night, for when Goldsborough friends and relations came, they stayed on as long as it pleased them to do so. There were so many Goldsboroughs in the immediate family that a few more persons at table, or upon the veranda, or strolling through the old boxwoods were hardly noticed, any more than a chance Goldsborough in one of their households would have been unduly noted.

In the ballroom, festooned with streamers and the blossoms of late-summer daisies and cornflowers, the orchestra was delicately working its way through the staid strains of a quadrille, while the dancers, mostly youthful and dressed in their best, moved through their paces.

Against the walls, a collection of dowagers drowsed in the heat, or fanned themselves sharply, their eyes taking in every detail of who was dancing with whom, and how they comported themselves. Liveried servants in powdered wigs circulated through the room, bearing silver trays of sparkling wines and minted sugar water.

Among the chaperones was Miss Henrietta herself, very becomingly attired in a gown of lavender embroidered silk, her salt-and-pepper locks covered by a brocade turban. She had been an acclaimed beauty in her youth, as her Sully portrait in the dining room would attest, and as the colonel was fond of telling her, she was still a great belle.

With only half an ear, she was listening to her cousin, Mrs. Maria Steptoe of The Anchorage, describing the confinement of her granddaughter, for even as she was furiously fanning herself her eye was upon her daughter, and her thoughts were uneasy.

Miss Sarah Goldsborough, having attained nineteen years without accepting any of the numerous offers of marriage that had come her way, was, in her mother's anxious opinion, well on her way to becoming an old maid.

Tall as her brothers, with the fair coloring and strawberry-blond hair of the Goldsborough side of the family, she was not the beauty that Miss Henrietta had been, having far too much of her father about her. And yet she was possessed of some sparkle, some charm that seemed to make the boys (for so they appeared to Miss Henrietta) scramble about her.

Right now, she was moving sedately enough through the measures of the entirely appropriate quadrille with the eminently eligible Buck Hudson, whose dark good looks and lean tallness made a charming contrast to her fairness. But her mother could see the restlessness in her daughter's eyes and had the distinctly uneasy feeling that Sally was about to go off on one of her starts again.

It was not that Sally was ever precisely hoydenish or that she did anything that one might call vulgar or immodest, Miss Henrietta reflected with a grateful sigh. It was simply that she frequently took a notion into her head, and nothing could shake her of it. It was, her mother supposed, a consequence of being outrageously spoiled by a doting father and four older brothers, but one could wish that one of those boys would snag her heart before she really took a start into her head.

Watching as Sally said something to Buck Hudson and left him standing alone on the floor, threading her way neatly through the dancers in her butter-yellow muslin gown, a wreath of flowers in her hair, Miss Henrietta ceased listening to her cousin entirely, closing her fan with a snap.

Sally said something to the orchestra leader, and the man nodded, making motions to the musicians. In a second, the decorous quadrille was replaced with a lively fiddler's jig, and with a smile of triumph, Sally returned to the dance floor, swirling about with Buck Hudson in the, to Miss Henrietta's mind, quite vulgar strains of a country dance better suited to farmers and watermen than a ball at Water Garden.

But the young people were enjoying it, forming the rounds as if they were at a barn dance rather than a ball, and clapping out the rhythm, calling the figures.

With a sigh, Miss Henrietta opened her fan again.

When the dance was over, Sally stood laughing and applauding, barely noticing that she was suddenly surrounded by several young men, all claiming that she had promised the next dance to them.

"I thank you very much," she said in her clear, rather drawling way, "but I promised my father that I would give him a dance, and that means I shall have to go and drag him away from the punch bowl and the war talk."

Buck Hudson grasped her gloved hand, his dark eyes burning into her own. "I shall accompany you," he insisted.

Another woman might have been thrilled to stroll about with Buck Hudson, but Sally, who had known him since they had been placed in the same cradle, merely smiled and shook her head as she extricated her hand from his. "Whyn't you offer Maranatha Cummings a dance?" she suggested. "She's been looking at you all evening."

Buck shrugged. But the music was starting again, and Miss Cummings, a prettily diminutive young lady with a good dowry was standing right there with a wreath of roses in her hair, so what was a fellow to do?

Picking up her demitrain, Sally threaded her way out of the ballroom and down the hallway. The night was unbearably close, and she opened her yellow chicken-skin fan to wave at herself, hoping to catch a breeze.

The syllabub bowl was placed in the study, where Col. Goldsborough and his cronies could smoke their pipes and cigarillos while they argued politics without annoying the womenfolk. The lower the syllabub went in the bowl, the louder their voices would become, and the more the room would fill with smoke, Sally thought, rather amused as she paused in the doorway and looked at her father and his cronies.

"The British have put a foraging party ashore," someone was saying, and Sally peered through the smoke to see an officer of the militia, still holding a long rifle under one arm, slightly out of breath. "They must be low on food and stores, for they tried to raid the henhouse over at Wembly Farm—"

"Damned limeys! What next?" someone muttered darkly, and there were mumbles of assent all around.

"It's not enough that they're blockading the entire bay so that we have to run our tobacco out of here like a pack of cursed smugglers—"

"And run in our sugarcane and rum," someone else said angrily.

"Now they've got to come ashore and try to steal our food. God knows but what they might try to attack our women or steal our slaves—"

"I don't think they'll get this far, gentlemen," said the militia man. "We've got troops out combing the woods looking for them, but we think they turned tail and made it back to that accursed sloop before we could catch 'em."

"Ought to hang every single one of them," Col. Goldsborough growled, quite red in the face. As a hero of the Revolution, and a thrice-elected member of the Senate, his anti-British feelings were well known. He drew heavily on his pipe. "Well, d'you wish me to gather up every able-bodied man here and organize a searching party?" He looked, Sally thought, as if hunting the British were a very great treat.

The militia man shook his head. "No need for that, Colonel. As I say, I don't think they'll get this far. We frightened them off. I only thought you ought to know, to be on your guard, should they try it again."

The colonel nodded, thrusting his heavy jaw out in a bulldoglike manner. "They'd better know not to come to Water Garden, damned Britshers! They'll find a buckshot welcome here!"

Sally opened her eyes very wide. Here was news indeed, she thought. She had often wondered about the shabby little sloop that had been standing out in the Santimoke for the past six months, and wondered what those British sailors aboard her must be thinking about them. This was as real as this war had ever been to her, and she was suddenly afraid.

"Sally! What are you doing here, my girl?" the

colonel suddenly asked, and all the men turned to look at her. "Don't you concern yourself with this, and for God's sake, don't tell your mother, or she'll be terrified that we've been invaded. Go and fetch your brothers, though—but no word to your sister-in-law. I want no upsets for Susannah, not in *her* condition." He softened his words with a wink.

Bemused, Sally could only nod and glide away, turning this news over in her head.

Save for Jonathan, who was in the ballroom dancing with Susannah, she could safely assume that Charles, William, and Henry were either congregated at the stables with their friends, where they would drink rum and examine all the finer points of their horses, or in the dining room attacking that vast cornucopia of food before heading for the ballroom to pick out all the prettiest girls with whom to dance.

Moving noiselessly on the hall rug, she thrust her head into the dining room.

It was empty of everyone, including servants, save for a person with his back to her who seemed to be entirely preoccupied with ripping the leg off a roasted turkey with his bare hands.

Sally was quite used to encountering strangers at Water Garden, for one never knew who her father might carelessly choose to invite to share their hospitality. But no one could she think of would come to their house who did not know how to remove a turkey leg with a knife and carving fork.

Too, there was something about the cut of his coat she did not like, even from the back. It had a distinctly military cut, was made of blue superfine, and capped with a pair of gold epaulettes quite unlike anything she had seen on the uniforms of their friends and acquaintances in the military. Nor did a gentleman attend an evening party wearing white knee britches and white stockings, Sally thought.

Suspicions were beginning to form in her mind. But of course, *that* was ridiculous.

Or was it?

She watched, fascinated, as he scooped up a jam tart, cramming it into his mouth, followed by several pieces of corn bread and a thick slice of ham.

It no longer seemed ridiculous at all. The question was, what to do about it? He had a rather nasty-looking pistol protruding from the waistband of his trousers, so screaming for help was quite likely to result in something unpleasant happening. On the other hand, if she went back up the hall—it was only twenty feet or so, but it might have been a mile at that moment—he might likely be gone through the same window he had obviously used to gain access to the veranda.

A lesser woman than Sally Goldsborough might simply have swooned away as a solution, but Sally Goldsborough had never fainted in her life and she had no intention of starting now, when things were becoming more interesting than they had been in months and months.

Imagine watching a British naval officer of some sort making a hog of himself at your birthday party! She might have been amused had it not occurred to her that he must be starving to eat like that, to take the risk he was taking.

She squared her shoulders resolutely. It seemed to her that there was one solution to the matter. Miss Henrietta would be furious, of course, but Sally could see that she had no other choice.

Treading noiselessly on her soft kid slippers,

Sally eased herself along the wainscoting of the dining room and picked up one of her mother's prized Imari pedestal vases from the mantelpiece.

Holding her breath, she inched her way across the room toward the Britisher and lifted it high above her head.

Since she was nearly as tall as he, it took no great effort to bring it down squarely on his head.

With a little sigh, as if to say "I expected something like this," he sank to the floor, still clutching his turkey leg.

Sally studied him for a moment. Somehow, she rather expected all the British to be of monstrous mien.

This one was rather handsome.

It was a great deal too bad.

2

The Santimoke County Jail was a square brick structure attached to the Santimoke County Courthouse. Primarily, it had in the past housed various drunkards, horse thieves, runaway slaves, and other odds and ends of an agrarian and orderly country society.

Never before had it housed an actual British prisoner of war, let alone one so obviously well-bred, young, handsome, and gentlemanly as the lieutenant, the Right Hon. Peter Marchman, R.N., who had awakened to find himself languishing in a single cell in that edifice, with a blinding headache and a strong feeling that he was in for it now, particularly when he discovered that his ship, the *Eagle*, had joined the invasion fleet that had burned the capital and shelled Fort McHenry in Baltimore. Logically, he assumed that this left him without hope of exchange for some hapless American captured by his countrymen. After receiving such a piece of news as the destruction of their Washington City and the attempted destruction of another important port, Mr. Marchman was fairly certain that it was more likely he would be hanged than paroled, and he settled back in his cell to read a stack of religious tracts provided by his jailer's wife while awaiting his fate.

Being of a philosophical turn of mind and inured to boredom by six months' service on the most blackened and hogged scow in the Royal Navy, he was about to give himself over to composing his gallows speech, all nobility and good advice, such as he had once seen delivered by a condemned highwayman at Tyburn in his Cambridge days, when he noticed that in addition to the various authorities who periodically came to question him, there had begun, in the first few days, to be a number of young belles who came in twos and threes bearing baskets of food, novels of the sort that young girls were likely to read, and an avid curiosity regarding his home and his history.

Although Mrs. Gutherie, the jailer's wife, provided him with three ample and excellent meals a day, Peter Marchman was not the man to refuse a gift of food, nor even the most dreadful gothic novel, particularly if it were presented to him by a pretty young miss in sprig muslin and a chipstraw bonnet, all agog to see the captured Britisher.

Had he known that rumor was spreading of his dark-haired, blue-eyed handsomeness, his gentlemanly manners, and his alien charm, he would have been embarrassed, for at twenty-three, Peter Marchman, whatever his faults, was sublimely unaware of his physical attractiveness for the opposite sex.

Resigned to the tangle his own impetuousness had landed him in, he thought that these county belles had only come to see the lion, and rather thought that he knew what Kean must feel like emerging from the stage door at Covent Garden.

Finding himself, however, *in* this tangle, Peter

saw no alternative to making the best of it. His cell was not uncomfortable, certainly not as uncomfortable as the cramped cabin he had shared aboard the *Eagle* with two midshipmen; the food was far, far better; and after six months on salt pork, hardtack, and watered rum, Mrs. Gutherie's corn bread and ham was ambrosia. Paradise was that that good lady had his linen laundered once a week and had even allowed him to use the pump in the jail yard to wash and shave himself as best he could. While he waited for his fate to be decided, Peter Marchman made the best of things, observing the Americans with as much curiosity as they were observing him.

He had been a prisoner for a fortnight when fate intervened, and when it did, it was in the person of a lady.

"Well, Mr. Marchman," said Gutherie one afternoon as Peter was lying on his bunk, staring out at the small patch of blue sky he could see through the window of his cell and digesting a lunch of cold crab, chicken, raspberry tart, and small ale. "You've got a visitor." Mr. Gutherie, who was not without a sense of humor, chuckled as he placed the visiting stool by the bars of Peter's cell. "A lady visitor who, I think, you've met afore. There you go, Miss Sally. Should you need anything, I'll be a shake away."

"Thank you, Mr. Gutherie," said a drawling voice, and with a rustle of petticoats, a young lady in a white muslin round dress and a very charming straw hat ornamented with yellow ribbons seated herself gingerly on the stool outside the bars, folding her gloved hands in her lap and staring at Mr. Marchman with brown eyes, framed by quite the longest lashes he had ever seen.

From beneath her hat, reddish-yellow curls framed a heart-shaped face, and a smattering of freckles decorated her delicate complexion.

Mr. Marchman swung himself off his bunk and struggled to his feet. "How do you do, ma'am?" he asked, feeling something quite novel in the way in which his heart seemed to be pounding in his chest. "I hope you will forgive my dishevelment—" He made a gesture about his cell, filled with baskets, flowers, and other tokens from his admirers.

"I am Sarah Goldsborough," the young lady said, not mincing matters, but assessing Mr. Marchman in quite the same way he had assessed her.

"I wish that I could say that your name was known to me," Peter said, "but I fear quite the opposite is true." Another one come to see the lion, he thought wryly. But, ah, the lion would like to see you, Miss Goldsborough!

Sally bit her lower lip. "We did not precisely meet, Lieutenant—"

"Mister. In the Royal Navy, lieutenants are addressed as Mister What's-his-face, or whatever. But I wish you would call me Peter," he added a trifle recklessly.

"We did not precisely *meet*, Mr. Marchman," Sally said again, twisting her reticule strings through her fingers and taking a deep breath. "I broke one of my mother's favorite Imari vases over your head." Her eyelashes dropped and two faint spots of crimson appeared in her cheeks.

"You?" Peter asked, his dark eyebrows raising toward his black curls. "My dear Miss Goldsborough!" A smile curved his lips. This was better than better, he thought, bowing deeply. If he could have reached her hand, he would have kissed it.

"I! Or is it me?" Sally cried, a little agitated. "I have not precisely come to apologize, Mr. Marchman. After all, you ruined my birthday ball." She shot him a flashing brown-eyed look.

"I must apologize myself. I am not generally in the habit of intruding where I am not invited, you know," Peter replied quickly, his blue eyes sparkling with mischief. "But there were, er, circumstances that drove me to desperation."

"Doubtless," Miss Goldsborough said a little tartly, determined not to encourage this strange Britisher in his deplorable levity, which was making her want to laugh, not at all the effect she wanted to make. Her friends had all raved to her about his looks and his manners, but she had not quite expected her own reaction to be as weak-kneed as theirs. With a little effort, she composed herself. "No, I cannot apologize, Mr. Marchman. You are an enemy of my country and an intruder in my father's house. I did what I thought best."

"Naturally. You acted with great resourcefulness, Miss Goldsborough," Mr. Marchman said with only the faintest trace of lightness in his voice. "But I must tell you, being hit with an Imari vase is hardly the most pleasant experience."

"My mother had strong hysterics over the loss of that vase," Sally retorted only half-seriously. "She was more upset over that than a Britisher sneaking into the dining room."

"But it was the food, you see," Mr. Marchman said, suddenly serious. He paced the length of his cell, adjusting the stock of his tunic. "I was so hungry, and lost in your accursed wilderness, separated from my men. Our provision ship from Tangier Island was three weeks late. Another day and we would have been reduced to eating the ship's rats. It was my idea to form a foraging party and come ashore. And believe me when I tell you, ma'am, that we were as afraid of you as you must have been of us. It was our intention to try to bag some game, a deer, at worst, to raid a henhouse on some lonely farm. We meant no harm to anyone, we were only hungry. One way or another, I became separated from my men. I must have wandered about in those accursed marshes for hours in the dark, certain sure that at any moment I would be set upon by Indians or rended by a bear—but why do you laugh?"

Miss Goldsborough shook her head. "Mr. Marchman, the last Indians left the Eastern Shore a hundred years ago. And I seriously doubt that there has ever been a bear in these parts."

Mr. Marchman shrugged. "Well, how was I to know?" he asked a trifle irritably. "When I bought my commission in the R.N., I thought I would be fighting Boney with Nelson, not stuck on some rotting sloop with a drunken captain and a half-witted crew in some godforsaken outpost of the New World, involved in a stupid and unsporting war—"

"Perhaps, Mr. Marchman, we ought to agree not to argue politics. Even if our countries seem unable to get along, I believe that we ought to make some effort to reach an understanding."

Peter nodded, acknowledging the wisdom of what she said. He had a strong feeling that he would make no headway with a lady who would be at daggers drawn with him concerning a useless war.

Sally must have been thinking along the same lines, for she propped her chin in her hand and looked up at him with those enormous eyes from beneath her hat brim. "You were telling me how you came to be making a glutton of yourself in our dining room," she said.

Marchman pushed a hand through his dark curls. "Yes, I was, wasn't I?" he asked, then shrugged, pushing his hands into his pockets. "I heard the music and I saw the lights, and I headed in that direction, looking, I suppose, for a bloody henhouse. I was hardly prepared to see your estate—that magnificent white house, with its galleries and verandas, filled with people who were laughing and talking and dancing and ... eating. It was hunger, Miss Goldsborough, that drove me on. In short, when the coast was clear of partygoers and servants and whatnot, I shimmied over the rail, climbed through the window, and fell upon the feast. I meant to be gone before anyone detected me, of course, but"—he smiled and shrugged—"you caught me, hit me, and made me your prisoner."

"Exactly so," Sally murmured thoughtfully.

"It is a very dreadful thing to be hungry," Mr. Marchman said.

"It does not appear as if you're starving now," Sally noted dryly.

Mr. Marchman looked at the brass buttons on his white waistcoat, bulging slightly from a fortnight's feasting, and sighed. "No," he agreed.

"Well"—Sally's voice was brisk, as she stood up, smoothing her gloves—"I came to ascertain that you were all right, and it would seem to me that you are. The Gutheries are good people, so I know that they are not abusing you. I only want you to know that I am not generally in the habit of smashing vases over people's heads."

"As I said before, Miss Goldsborough, I think you are a lady of great resourcefulness," Mr. Marchman said, and bowed.

"Have you had any word about what they've decided to do about you?" she asked casually, examining the ribbons on her hat.

Peter jerked his head toward the window of his cell. "When I hear them erecting the gibbet, I suppose I will know," he said lightly.

She looked at him. For the first time her expression lost its composure. "They would not do that," she exclaimed.

Peter shrugged. "I believe there is a custom in this country wherein a mob may take the law into its own hands? After the defeats at Washington and Baltimore, I may not be considered the most beloved person in your county."

"Lynching, it's called," Sally said impatiently, "and I believe the custom was imported from your country, Mr. Marchman. No, I rather assumed that you would sue for a parole."

Mr. Marchman shrugged. "It would seem that the nabobs of your county must decide upon that. However pleasant the Gutheries might be, and however comfortable these quarters, I am still a prisoner. And that cannot be a pleasant situation under any circumstances."

"No," Miss Goldsborough agreed. "But in parole, you would still be a prisoner, you know."

"Under parole, Miss Goldsborough, I should give my word as an officer and a gentleman that I would not attempt to escape or to aid my countrymen. I should be released into the custody of some respectable person who would make it his duty to give me room and board. I could not be out of uniform, for to do so would leave me open to charges of espionage, and my movements would be confined to a designated area laid out by my custodian, and by God, ma'am, it would be confining, but even this is better than rotting in one of Boney's prison hulks."

"I must go. My father thinks that I am at the mantua maker's. If he knew I was here, I think he would be angry with me. Good day, Mr. Marchman," Sally said briskly, and was gone before he could respond, her flat kid slippers whispering on the stone floor.

He lay back down again upon his bunk and stared up at the window, where just that patch of blue was visible through the iron bars.

"Miss Sarah Goldsborough," he said dreamily, enjoying the sound of her name as it rolled off his tongue.

The Americans were turning out to be a great deal more civilized than he had had any reason to suppose. Of course, he had never given much thought to America at all until he found himself on a ship bound for that New World across the ocean. But there was certainly a great deal to be said for these erstwhile colonials when they could produce females as attractive as these Santimoke County belles, in particular, Miss Sarah Goldsborough.

He drifted away into reverie, and from reverie into a pleasant nap, in which he dreamed that he was dancing with Miss Goldsborough in the ballroom at Marchman Place, far across the Atlantic, nestled in the rolling hills of the West Country. It would have been a wonderful dream if someone had not been banging at the great old oak door . . .

Banging.

With a start, Peter awakened and looked out the window.

Silhouetted against the blue sky, he saw the gallows being erected, and a cold hand clutched his heart.

3

"Well, sirrah! Awaken, I say, sirrah."

Someone was shaking Peter from his uneasy sleep, and he turned over to regard a large man, as tall as himself, with a strong, square face, crimson at this moment, bending over him, shaking his shoulder none too gently.

Peter yawned, sitting up. "Have you come to hang me, then?" he asked with considerably more bravado than he was feeling.

"Hang you? Hang you?" the large gentleman asked indignantly. "If I had my way, you'd be hanged all right and tight long ago, sirrah."

Over the large man's shoulder, Gutherie's face appeared in the morning gloom. "Hang you, Mr. Marchman? That's a very good joke, I must say! No, the colonel here has come to parole you out."

"Sign these papers and pack up your things, lad. I haven't got all day, you know." The colonel thrust papers and pencil into Peter's hands and stomped away, muttering.

Peter squinted at the papers and found that they were indeed releases of parole. He scribbled his signature upon these documents, hastily gathered up his few possessions, and with only a little shudder, walked through the open door of his cell and down the narrow corridor, going toward what unknown fate . . . He did not care to venture a guess.

The gentleman known as the colonel was waiting for him impatiently. "Well, hurry on, lad. Haven't got all day, you know," he said gruffly to Peter. "The trap's waiting outside."

Mrs. Gutherie was dabbing at her eyes with the corner of her apron, and the bluff old jailer himself held out a hand to Peter. " 'S been a real pleasure to have you with us, Mr. Marchman," he said quite seriously. "We usually don't shelter people of your class here."

"I've noticed," Peter said, bowing to kiss Mrs. Gutherie's work-worn hand.

"Oh, Mr. Marchman," she sighed, patting him in a quite maternal way, dabbing at a stain on his tunic with a corner of her apron. "Now you take care. I know that the colonel and Miss Henrietta will treat you right."

"Hurry on, sirrah! Haven't got all day," bellowed the colonel, and Peter, blinking in the sunlight, ran through the doorway, climbed up into the pony trap in the courtyard, and held his bundle in his lap.

"Geeyah," said the colonel to the horse, and the old beast snorted contemptuously as it picked up the shafts and lurched down the street.

" 'Send the barouche,' she says, 'send the barouche after the Britisher, or he'll think we're not hospitable, not hospitable at all.' Ha! I say! The trap's good enough for him, and I won't have the coachman taken away from his other duties because I have to drive all the way into Watertown and pick up some demmed Britsher, ha!"

"Yes, sir," Peter murmured, since it seemed that the colonel was expecting some sort of reply.

The American gentleman snorted, a sound amazingly like that of his horse. "The barouche, indeed! Well, young man, first and last, you've cost me a great deal of time and trouble. Lucky for you that my cousin is a judge, or you'd be sitting in the jail until this damned war is over, young man," he said gruffly. "Mind you keep those papers on you at all times, lest you be hung for spying."

"Yes, sir," Peter said, docile as he looked about himself at this morning illuminated by sunlight, with all of this flat country abloom with summer.

As they made their way out of town, red brick and white frame gave way to green fields, fields that seemed both vast and prosperous to Peter's English eyes. Truly, this America *was* a rich country, he thought.

The colonel tugged impatiently at his neck-cloth. Although the morning was already sweltering, he wore a brown broadcloth coat in a fashion a decade out of date in England and a pair of buckskin breeches. His boots had neither the shine nor the style of those to be found on any London gentleman of quality; indeed, they showed traces of mud, as if he had been out striding through the fields at daybreak. But for his accent, he might have been for all the world a country squire in Devon, Peter thought, taking home a paroled American officer from the Devonshire prison riots of last year.

Although Peter had a hundred questions he wanted to ask, he held his tongue, for it seemed to him that the colonel was in a taking, and the less he teased the gentleman, the better it would go for him in the long run.

Therefore, he sat docilely enough on the narrow seat of the trap and looked all about himself on the dusty and rutted road, at fields and rivers and the occasional grand plantation house they passed.

"Women," the colonel muttered to himself, or to Peter; Mr. Marchman was never quite certain which. "Softhearted creatures! Let him rot in jail, I say, where he'll get three meals a day and every girl in the county coming to visit with baskets of food and bouquets of flowers and God only knows what sort of geegaw things that women take into their heads to hand out. But, oh, no, she must feel guilty, she cannot rest worrying about the Britisher in the Santimoke County Jail. And her mother's just as bad, wringing her hands and moping about! Softhearted, that's what women are!"

"Yes, sir," Mr. Marchman said politely.

"How do you think I got to be a colonel, sirrah, I ask you? Was it by dint of hard labor, or was it by settin' back on the veranda and watching others fight the fine and glorious Revolution? Independence and liberty, that's what I said." The colonel thumped his chest with the stock of his whip. "Independence and liberty for all! I'll have no British tyranny upon my back, tax my tobacco! So I fought, in the Fourth Maryland, and so I became a colonel when I wasn't much more than your age, young man."

The colonel peered into Mr. Marchman's face. "So don't go about thinking that I have any great love for you or your countrymen, sirrah, because I don't!"

"Yes—I mean, no, sir," Peter said.

The colonel's beetle brows drew together. "And here's more! I am a hawk, sirrah, a hawk upon this war! Free trade and sailor's rights, say I, and no two ways about it. Do you see Boney pressing honest American lads off good American ships, hey?"

"No, sir," Peter said.

"There, you see? So we won't have any of that around my dinner table. Makes me dyspeptic! I'm a man as brooks no contradictions in my own home!"

"Yes, sir," Peter murmured.

The colonel nodded. "Glad that we have that straight at least. As long as we understand each other, there'll be no trouble until it comes to ransom or exchanging you. Don't suppose you have any skills, hey?"

"I took a first at Cambridge in history, sir," Peter said mildly. "I have, of course, all the requisite nautical skills, I am literate, I have some skill in agriculture, animal husbandry, and the like—"

"William and Mary man myself," the colonel admitted. "Agriculture and animal husbandry, you say? That we can always use. Have you ever read law?"

"No, sir."

"Pity. My youngest son's cramming to read for the bar. You might help his elder brother, though; he's to go to William and Mary, and he's more interested in fast horses and languid women than his books." The colonel seemed visibly cheered by this news of his parolee's education and skill. "Well, at least you won't be a drain upon us; we'll find plenty to keep you busy and occupied and out of Britisher trouble."

"It would seem so, sir."

"And away from the womenfolk," the colonel continued, his mood turning black again. "This paroling of you may have been the harebrained idea of my daughter and my wife, but as long as you are under my roof, sirrah, you will comport yourself as a gentleman should, else you'll have me and my daughter's four brothers to be answering after, you understand?" To emphasize his point, the colonel prodded Peter with his whipstock, scowling so fiercely that the younger man drew away, rather alarmed.

"Yes, sir," Mr. Marchman said. "Colonel, I *am* a gentleman," he added. It began to occur to him that this man's wife and daughter had beseeched his parole for reasons he preferred not to contemplate too closely. Doubtless, the daughter was as her father, in which case it would certainly be easy enough to drift away from her direction. Particularly with the five, no *four* brothers all breathing down his neck.

He sighed. Four was enough. He hoped that the war would be over soon.

They rode the rest of the way in silence, or as much silence as the colonel was capable of, for, from time to time, he would comment upon the state of the tobacco crop or the condition of a field, which gave Mr. Marchman to understand, not without a certain degree of awe, that the colonel owned a great deal of land, as much as might make up two estates in England, and again, he was impressed with the sheer size of this new country into which he had come.

"Well, then, here we are," said the colonel at last, turning the cob in between two large brick gateposts and up a shady lane lined with old poplar trees.

The white house ahead looked vaguely familiar to Mr. Marchman, but he dismissed the thought. Surely, there must be a dozen white houses in this county that sat upon the river with shady verandas and neat balconies.

Surely, there must be . . .

He shaded his eyes with his hand as a moving figure to his left caught his eye. A magnificent Arabian was galloping across the field, handled expertly by a woman in a celestial-blue habit. He held his breath as she came to a tide ditch, but the horse cleared it with such grace of motion that he almost wanted to applaud the horse—and the rider's skill.

"Magnificent," he said aloud.

"Isn't she just?" There was a great deal of pride in the colonel's voice. "That is my daughter."

In spite of himself, Peter's interest was piqued. Even if she was as bracket-faced as her father, what a bruising rider she was! Perhaps it would not be all that bad, after all.

The daughter was riding up the lane, some thirty or forty yards ahead of them, her mount kicking up the dust behind.

At the entrance to the house, she reined in, the horse dancing delicately on its hooves as a stable-hand tried to grasp the bridle. She turned and looked down the lane, watching the trap and its occupants approaching, from a very good seat.

It was difficult for Peter to see through the dusty clouds she had stirred up, but it was beginning to dawn upon him that there, after all, was more hope than he had even dreamed of before this moment. He dared not allow himself to believe—

But it was.

"Well, Sally, my dear," the colonel was calling as they approached, "here's your Britisher, all right, tight and paroled. I hope that you and Miss Henrietta will be happy and let an old man rest."

Sally Goldsborough looked down at Mr. Marchman from beneath a very rakish blue broadcloth cap, set at a jaunty angle on her strawberry curls. Was Peter mistaken, or did she drop the slightest of winks in his direction as she extended a gloved hand?

"How do you do, Mr. Marchman? Welcome to Water Garden," she drawled. "I hope that we shall be able to make you comfortable here."

"I am certain that you will," Mr. Marchman replied, holding her hand just a little longer than necessary.

"Colonel? Colonel? Are you home, my dear?"

Mr. Marchman turned to see a small lady in sprigged muslin, a charming lace cap set upon her salt-and-pepper curls, emerge from the doorway.

"Home, indeed, Miss Henrietta," boomed the colonel, springing easily down from the trap and up the steps to take his wife's hand in his own. "And I have brought your Britisher with me, my love."

Mr. Marchman reluctantly let go of Sally Goldsborough's hand and climbed down from the trap.

"Er"—Col. Goldsborough shuffled through his pockets and produced some papers—"Miss Henrietta Goldsborough, my life and my wife, may I present Mr. Peter Marchman?"

"Well, I am charmed, I am sure," fluttered Miss Henrietta. "I really didn't get to meet you when—well, you know."

Peter was utterly charmed as he took her small hand in his own and bowed. "I must beg your forgiveness, Mrs. Goldsborough, for my unfortunate intrusion the evening of your ball. Fortunes of war, you know."

"You must call me Miss Henrietta, for everyone does," she said while the colonel beamed down upon her fondly. "Isn't that right, Colonel?"

"That's the way of it. The boys are about somewhere, and my daughter-in-law—"

"Susannah's resting. Her delicate condition," Miss Henrietta said, flapping her hands suggestively in the air.

The colonel nodded. "Well, time enough to meet them all later. Daresay they're curious enough to have a look at the man their sister brained—"

"With my best Imari vase! I shall never find another to match it," Miss Henrietta said, as if British officers were bashed in her home as a matter of course. "Well, I imagine you would like to see your room. I hope the Gutheries treated you kindly? Good, they are nice people, aren't they? She was a Wallace, you know—"

"Mama, it appears that Father is dying for his julep," Sally drawled, still upon her horse. "Why don't you take him in? I'll show Mr. Marchman his room."

"Oh, yes, your julep," Miss Henrietta fluttered, thrusting her tiny hand into the crook of her husband's enormous arm. "Come along, Colonel, my dear, and I'll see that you're comfortable."

The colonel looked as if he had something to say to Mr. Marchman, but Miss Henrietta had a will of iron and he already was in the house.

"Would you hand me down, Mr. Marchman?" Sally asked.

"Miss Sally, the mounting block's right there," said the stablehand, a young man not yet possessed of a romantic turn of mind.

"Quite all right, my lad," Peter said, lifting Miss Goldsborough down from her sidesaddle.

"You can just take those horses to the stables. I shall see that Miss Sally is all right."

Since Mr. Marchman gave no outward indications of the barbaric qualities reputed to belong to the British enemy, Sam took horse and trap and led them slowly back toward the stableyard, glancing over his shoulder from time to time to see if horns or fangs were growing.

Happily for them, neither Sally nor Peter was aware that he was the object of much curiosity at Water Garden.

Lightly, setting her upon her feet, Peter realized that she was nearly as tall as he.

They stood and stared at each other, smiling for several seconds.

Finally, Peter spoke. "Miss Goldsborough, I hope that you will do me the honor of marrying me."

Sally threw back her head and laughed. "Of course, Mr. Marchman, I should say it is *I* who am honored. You have but to name the date and see my father."

"Yes, your father," Peter repeated. "And four brothers."

She looked at him. "Why, you're serious," she exclaimed.

Peter regarded her with his pale-blue eyes. "Miss Goldsborough, I have never been more serious about anything in my life."

Sally opened her large brown eyes very wide. For the first time in her nineteen years, she was coy. "Well, Mr. Marchman, it would seem that we may have a great long time to discuss the matter, would it not? If you will come with me—"

"Ah, but I've asked and you've said yes," Peter interrupted, grinning at her. "The rest is simply courtship."

"Simply courtship," Miss Goldsborough repeated thoughtfully.

"And now that we've settled that, would you please show me to my room? I'm sorry I have no luggage, but in my position, one rarely packs a portmanteau, you know."

4

For Peter Marchman, reared by cold and brangling relations in an ancient and somewhat forbidding household, his first evening at Water Garden *en famille* was something of a revelation.

Whereas he had spent his childhood eating in polite silence, with much attention to manners, while the butler directed footmen with hand signals, here at Water Garden, there was no such thing as silence.

As a liveried butler passed enormous platters of ham, chicken, green beans, gravy, and India curry relishes to Col. Goldsborough, that gentleman loaded up Chinese export porcelain plates and passed them down the table. Everyone talked at once, the colonel the loudest, his voice booming out across the room in contrapuntal harmony to that of Miss Henrietta at the other end of the long Sheraton board.

"Butter beans, Pa, I hate butter beans—"

"Eat them anyway, William, as they are considered to be nourishing."

"I declare, I have the strangest craving, Miss Henrietta, for pickled beets. Do you think Cook might have any?"

"Pickled beets, pickled betters, was what we was wont to call 'em, and glad to have them were we, too, at Valley Forge—"

"Father's told that Valley Forge story a thousand times. Don't listen."

"So I took a couple of hands and went down to the lower acres on the marsh. It looked to me as if the tidewall had broken open, 'cause about a quarter acre around there was all covered up with saltwater. Have to send a crew down there to repair that dike."

"—decided to take that horse and race him after church on Sunday."

"Can I have more ham, Pa?"

"Give Susannah plenty of that chicken, Colonel. She's eating for two now."

"I wouldn't race that horse on a dare from the devil himself."

"Charles, we won't have any talk like that at the table, if you please. Mention the devil and he shall appear."

"Looks as if he already has," Charles said, wiping his mouth with his napkin and looking at Mr. Marchman suspiciously.

Peter inclined his head, as if he had been paid a compliment, and addressed himself to his plate. Instead of the overcooked beef and soggy vegetables that he was used to eating as a part of the English cuisine, everything was light and done to a turn.

"Charles, you take that back right now or else, when I see Marcie Tyler after church on Sunday, I'll tell her that you were out in the garden enjoying the moonlight with Lydia Steptoe last Tuesday night," Sally said across the table, eyeing her youngest brother fishily.

Charles Goldsborough flushed, dropping his eyes. "Sorry," he said.

"Sally is quite right," boomed Col. Goldsborough from the head of the table. "As long as Mr.

Marchman is with us, he is our guest, and is to be treated as a guest at Water Garden."

"Quite right, Colonel," Miss Henrietta said firmly, leaning to pat Peter's hand as he sat to her right. "Don't you pay any attention to what people say, young man. Especially my sons." She shook her head.

"Well," said Charles, his voice cracking, "it's only what everyone else is saying around here. The British are devils. They burned the capital and shelled Fort McHenry—"

"No politics at table," Colonel Goldsborough shouted, pounding his massive fist against the table so hard that it shook the plates and glasses.

While Susannah went on calmly eating pickled beets for two, the Goldsboroughs all began talking politics at once, and each and every one of them had a different opinion.

Peter ate his dinner and looked at them. Sally's four brothers were graded copies of their father. All of them were tall, fair-skinned and blond-haired, with their father's strong jaw and beetling brows. Jonathan, the eldest, was only a year older than himself, and was already expecting to become a father very shortly. Susannah, his wife, was quite advanced and, it seemed to Peter, ate enough to feed an entire regiment of increasing women. Her husband watched her with a particularly moonstruck expression, as if she had accomplished something quite extraordinary.

Charles and Henry were the ones that Peter supposed he was to tutor into university. He had only to look at them to know that the last thing either one of them wanted to be doing was poring over a book. Horses, sailing, and females were the things that interested them, just as that had been all that had really interested Peter at their ages.

William, he presumed, was the one who was to read law, for there was already something of the attorney about him, some look in his eyes that suggested that he was constantly weighing up the angles and figuring the advantages. Peter noticed that he was a sharp debater, and grew sharper with each tankard of dry ale that he consumed.

A most interesting family, he thought. It was rather as if there were so many of them that one extra person was barely noticed. In the course of the dinner, they seemed to open up and swallow him into their midst just as he guessed that they had swallowed the perpetually hungry Susannah, who managed to polish off no less than three slices of apple pie for dessert and still had room for several pieces of fruit from the centerpiece.

Seated opposite him, between two brothers, Sally captured most of his attention. Even though the evening was sweltering, she seemed cool and elegant in a thin white muslin gown, ornamented only by a bodice of tiny Van Dyke point-de-Venice lace and a lavender sash. A string of tiny pearls depended from her neck, just resting against the curve of her breasts, and her strawberry-blond hair was caught in a Psyche knot at the crown of her head. She never would have passed muster at a fashionable London table, but there was something achingly charming about her in Peter's eyes.

She had not spoken to him since their amazing interview in the drive, and she had been cautious to avoid catching his eye all evening, but he was well aware that she was regarding him as much as he was regarding her, and just as covertly.

For the first time in his sometimes erratic career, Peter Marchman knew what he wanted. That the lady in question might not want the same thing did not enter his head. He was sure, even if she was not, that that gentleman known as the Creator had placed them upon the face of this earth for the sole purpose of bringing them together in this fashion. There really could be no other excuse for it, now that he gave it serious consideration; in the ordinary course of things he doubted that he would fall instantly in love with a lady who smashed an Imari vase over his head.

For her part, Miss Goldsborough, in general a rather prosaic-minded young lady, found herself in something of a whirl.

It had, of course, been her duty to visit the British officer in jail, since she had been the cause of his capture and confinement. News of his dark good looks, his devastating blue eyes, his British charm had of course reached her ears from her bosom friends, and she could not deny that such benign reports had influenced her decision. But she had not quite expected to come face to face with a man who could literally take her breath away.

It was certainly a new feeling for Sally. The only daughter of parents with four sons, she had been cosseted and made much of her entire life. Her father could deny her nothing and it had been for her sake only that the colonel had retrieved Mr. Marchman from confinement. Her brothers had protected her and at the same time, by their association, had given her a rather tomboyish, if not precisely masculine streak. Her mother had long ago despaired of making her into a lace-and-satin doll whose die-away manners and fluttering affectations were commonly held to attract beaux. And yet, Miss Goldsborough, since she had let down her skirts and put up her hair, had never lacked for suitors, most of them in every way eligible to claim Miss Sarah Goldsborough of Water Garden as a wife.

Truly, Miss Henrietta despaired of Sally's ever marrying. For she had rejected them, one and all, declaring that she was not in love. What there was not to love, Miss Henrietta could never quite see. Herself a reigning belle, she could view the opposite sex only in terms of persons to be conquered by beauty and charm. That Sally, having grown up surrounded by men, might see no mysteries—and hence no romance—in the sex had not occurred to her worried mother.

Indeed, until Mr. Marchman had stumbled into her life, Sally had resigned herself to a dwindling spinsterhood, gradually taking to mobcaps and the role of benevolent aunt to the masses of offspring she fully expected Jonathan and Susannah to produce, rather than marry for convenience.

Mr. Marchman. Miss Goldsborough stole yet another glance at the Englishman from beneath her lashes. Fancy, proposing to her after he had known her not above two hours!

She should have thought it comical; it was certainly a novel approach, she had to admit. But it certainly left one a little dazzled. He seemed so confident of his ability to win her.

Certainly, the Englishman was unlike anyone she had ever encountered before, and that, she had to admit, made him dangerously attractive to her.

She shook her head, as if she could dismiss such folly from her thoughts, attempting to concentrate upon her plate.

Having made up his mind that he would make Miss Goldsborough his lady, Peter was able to remark upon his surroundings with a great deal of interest. He had to admit that he was intrigued by these Americans and everything that surrounded them. He would have been less than human had he not noted the contrasts.

Marchman Place, his home in the West Country, was vast, dark, dank, and filled with the recollections of its great antiquity, the very air there seeming to him to be ossified by centuries of tradition and the rancor between his relations.

By contrast, Water Garden was light, open, and airy. The rooms were filled with windows that did not leak and looked out upon pleasant vistas. They were furnished by graceful examples of the work of Sheraton, Hepplewhite, and examples of the work of lesser-known, if no-less-talented American cabinetmakers from Newport and Philadelphia and Baltimore, and arranged in comfortable groupings. The halls were broad and airy, the polished floorboards laid with good Oriental rugs. Miss Henrietta would have died if the sheets on a bed in her house were damp or unaired, and the verandas were invitingly cool on hot summer afternoons. Peter was willing to bet that the colonel's chimneys never smoked and that in winter a fire was laid in every room. He was also reasonably certain that the roof at Water Garden never leaked and that icy blasts of winter wind did not howl through the chinks in the doors.

It was so completely different from the ramshackle pile in which he had been reared that he felt as if he could be living upon another planet.

One could become quite used to it all, Peter thought.

After dinner, as the family was repairing to the parlor, a string of guests passed by on their way home from Watertown. Apparently they were the family from the neighboring plantation, composed of a mother, a father, a grandmother, a rakish uncle with a mustache, and several married and unmarried sons and daughters, but it seemed to be enough excuse for the colonel to call for the punch bowl and the syllabub, and very soon, it appeared as if the Goldsboroughs were having a party.

The elder gentlemen took their pipes and their punch and retired to the veranda, to rock comfortably back and forth in the still of the evening and talk about planting and politics, while the ladies clustered in one end of the parlor, about the reclining form of Susannah on a chaise, a bowl of fruit close at hand, to gossip and chaperone the younger members of the gathering.

Jonathan was persuaded to dig out his fiddle, and Sally played the pianoforte while the rest of them made up sets and danced away the evening. Peter would have been content to stand adoringly by and turn the pages for Miss Goldsborough's music if he had had his own way, but Miss Goldsborough, a trifle roguishly, sent him away to dance a lively set of country reels with the Misses Jump, who were agog with curiosity over the captured Britisher.

With a woeful look, Mr. Marchman did as his hostess bid, and was duly charming to a trio of pudding-faced misses who could only simper and stare at him as if he were a lion or a giraffe in spite of his best efforts to be charming and live up to his reputation. But not too charming, of course; there were, after all, the Brothers Jump and the Brothers Goldsborough to watch him very carefully, lest his liberties be too foreign for American custom.

It was well past ten when, at the urgings of the Jump brothers, Miss Clarissa Jump was urged to replace Miss Goldsborough at the pianoforte, and Mr. Marchman was able to secure her hand for a country dance.

He was not disappointed by his wait, for Sally Goldsborough danced as well as she rode, and as they went through the figures, she smiled up at him in a most teasing way.

"Well, Mr. Marchman," said she, "I am sure that you must find us very dull after England."

"On the contrary, Miss Goldsborough, I am more than entranced with Yankee custom and style," Peter grinned.

Sally lifted her shoulders very slightly, as if to show her indifference, but a faint quivering at the corners of her lips betrayed her serious expression.

"Have you given any thought to the proposal I laid before you this afternoon?" Peter asked.

Sally cast a sideways look at him. "I have," she said calmly, turning about to bow in the figure of the dance toward him.

Peter executed a graceful bow of his own and resumed his possession of Miss Goldsborough's hand. "And?" he asked, trying not to sound too eager.

Her smile was radiant. "It would seem, Mr. Marchman, that I have a long, long, long time to think about it, does it not?"

There was no choice but to agree with her that she did.

It might be years before the war was over.

5

It was, in fact, a briskly cold day in early March when a militia man beat up the icy lane, hell for leather, toward Water Garden, bearing with him Gen. Hardy's greetings to Col. Goldsborough and the news that a treaty had been signed in Geneva in December between America and England.

"Peace," he cried, galloping past Miss Goldsborough and Mr. Marchman, who had been out riding over the snowy fields. "Peace! Peace!"

Mr. Marchman squared his shoulders beneath his borrowed coat, squinting against the sun as he watched the man dismount and rush up the steps of the house. "Peace," he said.

Miss Goldsborough shifted in the saddle, tilting the brim of her felt hat, the feathers rustling in the breeze. "Peace," she agreed. "Who won?"

"No one wins in a war," Mr. Marchman said, then grinned. "At least I may be rid of this damned tunic and back into mufti," he added with a rueful glance down at his much-patched and -darned naval officer's coat, sadly worn and quite shabby in spite of all of Miss Henrietta's best efforts at keeping it presentable. He reached out and placed a hand over one of Sally's. "We should go directly back, my dear. I would like to speak to the colonel and have it over with."

46

Sally grinned. "Yes, I daresay he will be in a mood with this news. Only this morning he was complaining that his tobacco was rotting in the warehouses because he could not ship."

"I suppose, coming on top of the news of the American victory at New Orleans, this will put the old fellow in alt," Marchman said hopefully.

"I should hope so," Sally replied thoughtfully, spurring her magnificent horse.

"Sally, my love, you have not changed your mind?" Peter asked, reining in beside her.

She gave him one of her radiant smiles. "My dear Mr. Marchman, we have been courting for eight months. Of course I want to marry you. Do you still want to marry me?"

"I never wanted anything more," Peter said reverently.

Sally nodded. "Then we are agreed?"

For answer, Peter leaned across their horses and gave her a kiss that took her breath away.

"Satisfied, my love?" he asked.

"Absolutely," she replied with a sigh, and they rode back toward the house.

"Peace," Col. Goldsborough was declaring to Miss Henrietta and the assembled company in the parlor, waving about the declaration in such a self-satisfied manner that one might have thought he had been present at the treaty table.

"Well, I declare," Miss Henrietta said vaguely, snipping a piece of thread from her embroidery. "Now we can get things back to normal around here," she added.

It was at that moment that Sally and Peter came into the room, their faces flushed from the cold. The colonel, who had never quite accustomed himself to the presence of Mr. Marchman in his household, frowned slightly at the English gentleman, but when he spoke, his tones were definitely those of toleration.

"Well, Mr. Marchman, you must know that peace has been declared anytime these past three months. You are a free man, sirrah. A free man! And this letter came for you with the declaration, I might add, yes, indeed."

Taking the sealed missive the colonel proffered him, Peter nodded, wasting no time in breaking the wax seal. It had been well over two years since he had heard from home, and he scanned the lines of the crossed and recrossed missive with an expressionless face.

"Peace," the colonel repeated loudly, and doubtless would have discoursed upon this theme for some time had not his daughter, who did not believe in mincing words, quickly spoken up.

"Father, Mr. Marchman would like to speak to you in your study," Sally said urgently, pressing her toe against her beloved's instep.

"Hey?" the colonel asked. "Speak with me in my study, hey? Is this so, Marchman?"

Mr. Marchman quickly folded his letter, thrusting it into an inner pocket. "Yes, sir. As soon as might be convenient," he said, meeting the colonel's suspicious gaze with clear blue eyes.

"Can't imagine what you'd want to say to me that can't be said in front of the family. No secrets between us, sirrah," the colonel said firmly. "However, no time like the present, I always say, so if you will come along with me, Mr. Marchman, we shall settle accounts, indeed."

With a single, speaking look at his beloved, Mr. Marchman shrugged his shoulders inside his shabby naval tunic and followed Col. Goldsborough's broad back through the double doors across the hall, closing them behind himself.

Still in her russet wool jersey habit, Sally sat down at the pianoforte and began, rather dreamily, to pick out a tune.

Miss Henrietta poked her needle in and out of the tambour frame several times before she gave up all pretense of handwork and exclaimed, "What can be taking them so long?"

"I am certain that Father is expressing a great many objections to the idea of my marrying Peter, Mother," Sally said calmly enough, even though her fingers were trembling slightly.

"Sarah Elizabeth Goldsborough, you could have had any man on the Eastern Shore, not to mention Annapolis or Baltimore!"

"But I decided that I wanted Peter, Mother."

"Why? Oh, this will upset your father no end."

"Why?" Sally smiled, a small, rather secret smile. "Because he is different, I suppose. Because I only had to look at him to know that he was the only man in the world for me, from the very first moment I saw him face to face. Besides, I think that one almost owes him that much after one had brained him with one of your good Imari vases." Sally smiled and turned away from the pianoforte to grasp her mother's hands. "Oh, can't you see? It was just that we could dance together, and we could ride out and sail, and he would hold my prayer book in church, and afterward, when we went to the races, we would stroll through the crowds together, and I felt so proud to be with him. I don't know, don't ask me to explain, save that I know that I love him and he loves me."

"But what will you do when you go all the way to England? It is so far away. . . ."

"Oh, Mother, we shall return from time to time, I know. It is far away, but I would go wherever Peter was."

"Oh, Sally, you are so young to be casting your future in such a reckless manner." Miss Henrietta fretted.

"Mother, you have been telling me these past three years and more that if I did not marry I would be an old maid," Sally pointed out patiently.

"Well, I did not think you would be marrying and going so far away," her mother sighed.

"Well, within a fortnight Susannah will be brought to bed and you will have a grandchild to take your mind off my problems," Sally countered. "Aside from which, you like Peter. You are always telling me that you do."

"Well, of course I like Peter! He is a very gentlemanly young man, and he has been quite a considerate houseguest. But to take you so far away. What did you say the name of his house was to be?"

"The family house is Marchman Place, and it is in Devon. But it is not Peter's house. He has an older brother, and *his* father is quite as healthy as Father. He has, oh, I forget how much a year, but we shall be quite comfortable, and there will be no need for me to touch my inheritance, which can be safely settled upon the grandchildren that Peter and I intend to present to you. That is, if Father gives his consent."

For the first time, a note of doubt crept into her voice. Sally could not marry without the consent of her parents under any circumstances. She would have considered such a step utterly treacherous, for she was dearly attached to Miss Henrietta and the colonel, and valued their love.

But she also knew that, as his only daughter, the colonel could deny her very little, even a husband that she was certain he would consider, at first, unsuitable in every way. She must simply trust in Peter's charm and his who-knew-what-a-many pounds a year to carry the day.

Still, it seemed an eternity to both women before the double oak doors of the study were opened. The colonel emerged, looking as if someone had drained him of blood.

"Jasper!" he shouted for the butler. "Whiskey punch, and quickly! A baron! The damned fella's a baron!"

Behind him, Peter emerged, a faint smile covering his lips. He winked at Sally, and she heaved a sigh of relief.

"Well, daughter," the colonel said, "if you insist upon marrying this young fool, then you may have him with my blessing. A baron!" He announced Peter's title as if it were on a par with being a highwayman.

Furious that he could think of no good reason why Sally should not marry Mr., well, now, Lord Marchman, for he could deny his daughter nothing that she wanted, Col. Goldsborough had given his consent. "But," he added, "I cannot help but mislike this business of being a baron, you know, hey?"

"A baron?" Miss Henrietta asked, impressed.

"A baron?" Sally repeated blankly, nonplussed. Peter had not mentioned titles, so very English to her mind.

He shrugged lightly. "I'm sorry," he said to her, "but it cannot be helped, you see. I am, alas, a baron." Peter handed Sally the letter he had received, and she scanned it.

"Oh, Peter, I am so sorry. Your father and

brother within months of each other—what a terrible shock it must be for you!"

Peter shrugged. "I had fallen out with my family so long ago that it is almost as if someone had announced the death of strangers. Will you still have me, even though I am a baron now and you must be Lady Marchman?"

"Of course," Sally said, but she could not like something about the coldness that had crept into his voice when he spoke of his family.

"Well, Peter," Miss Henrietta said, "you know that I am quite fond of you, and that I should welcome you as a son, but, oh, dear, it does quite remind one of Cousin Felicia running off with a dancing master."

"Just so, ma'am," Peter said quite seriously, taking her hand within his own and smiling down at her. "But I promise that I shall endeavor to make Sally as happy as I can, baroness or not."

"Well," said the colonel, quaffing his whiskey punch, "I suppose planning the wedding is in order. Holy Trinity and bridesmaids and what not?"

"As soon as possible, sir," Lord Marchman said. "It would appear that I must return to Marchman Place." He lifted his glass. "Would that my family were like the Goldsboroughs," he announced.

Part Two

Marchman Place, Devon—June 1815

6

A cool English rain had been falling steadily for the past twenty-four hours and looked to pour for the space of another twenty-four without remission.

The steady rhythm of droplets on the windows and the gusts of wind that periodically sent puffs of smoke wafting through the green salon precisely matched the rather gray mood of the three persons assembled in that shabby and cheerless room. That it was the warmest, as well as the most welcoming of all the various chambers in Marchman Place said a great deal about the upkeep and situation of that vast and ancient pile.

The ormolu clock on the mantel chimed, rather dyspeptically, twice, and the Roman-nosed matron who reclined amid a pile of cushions and a welter of shawls upon the somewhat sprung chaise longue, straightened her turban and reached for a vial amid the powders and potions on the tray that was rarely far from her side. Inhaling deeply of restorative camphor, she reclined again, emitting a heartier sigh than one would have expected from a self-proclaimed invalid.

"Wherever can Peter be? He should have arrived long ago," she fretted, closing her eyes as if the effort put out to make her query had exhausted her utterly.

"Come, now, Aunt Theresa," drawled a lazy voice from the window seat. "You know that it will take him forever to come up from Portsmouth in this dirty weather."

Mrs. Theresa Marchman cast a look at the speaker from over her cushions. "All very well for you, Gervais," she said in failing accents. "You do not have to depend upon Peter's goodwill to maintain your living at Marchman Place."

"No, and I thank God for that," Gervais Fallon said fervently. "Peter and I never *did* manage to scrape along. But as you can see, I am here to do my duty by the new head of the family." He crossed one elegantly trousered leg over the other. From the top of his pomaded locks to the tips of his gleaming Hessians, everything about him proclaimed the man of fashion. Gervais' resemblance to his cousin was very close, for he was possessed of the same dark coloring and startling blue eyes as Peter. But Peter would never have worn a waistcoat of bottle-green striped brocade, nor would he sport collar points so high that he could not turn his head. "Yes, nothing else could possibly drag me into the country save my duty to my dear coz," he drawled thoughtfully, picking up the dice box and shaking it.

"Nothing?" teased the young lady seated opposite him. Like her mother, she was dressed in the grays and whites of half-mourning, but even these somber hues could not quite diminish her very startling blond beauty. Ever since she had put up her hair and let down her skirts, she had been proclaimed not just beautiful, but a beauty, and of a consequence, there was something just a trifle spoiled about the delicate set of her lips and the manner in which she carried her slender figure.

"But of course, I also came to succor my lovely cousin Annabella. It cannot be great deal of enough to be buried in the country for a year and a half without anyone to tell you how lovely you are, my dear." Gervais' voice was lightly mocking, but Annabella was secure enough to accept the undercurrent of seriousness as her due. She was perfectly aware that for all of his devil-may-care attitude, Gervais, one of the fashionable world's most eligible catches, had remained single for her sake these many years.

"And I am very grateful to you, Gervais," she said, a ripple of laughter in her voice. "You have no idea how very disobliging one feels it to be when Uncle Robert and Cousin Richard drowned themselves in the middle of one's Season, making one come home and be locked away from everything exciting forever and ever!"

"Annabella!" Mrs. Marchman exclaimed, roused from her languor and much shocked.

But the beauty merely tossed her head. "Well, it is true, you know," she said defensively. "Besides, Uncle Robert and Cousin Richard were extremely unpleasant, always making Mama and me feel as if we were existing on charity."

"That much is true," Mrs. Marchman sighed. "Robert was always a singularly difficult brother-in-law."

"Uncle Robert was an odious wretch," Annabella confirmed. "A cheese-paring, miserly wretch. To think that he schemed and planned that I should marry Richard solely to keep my inheritance in the family."

"*I* would not tolerate that!" Mrs. Marchman roused herself enough to exclaim. "Every sensibility was offended, to see my Annabella foisted off upon that—that, well!"

"Loose fish, Aunt Theresa?" Gervais drawled. From an interior pocket in his cream-colored jacket of bath superfine, he withdrew an elegant gold snuffbox. With a practiced flick of his wrist, he opened the latch and applied a pinch of the mixture to either nostril.

"I said no such thing," Mrs. Marchman protested, resorting to her camphor at the very idea. "But in the end, I triumphed, and Richard was forced to open Marchman House for Annabella's Season, whether he liked it or not. And, oh, how he begrudged the outlay! If it had not been for Great-aunt Aurelia giving him the sharp side of her tongue, who knows what would have happened?"

"And then of course, Uncle and Richard had to go and spoil it all by going on that *stoopid* fishing trip on the River Clyde and getting themselves drowned. Oh, was it any wonder that Peter left the way he did?" Annabella exclaimed, casting a look out the window as if she expected to see her cousin coming up the drive at the minute.

"You of all people should understand the circumstances that sent Peter out to buy his commission," Gervais murmured innocently.

"Oh, Gervais, if one were not used to you always saying the worst of one—Uncle Robert and Peter quarreled dreadfully, and Peter quit the house. I had nothing to do with it." Did Annabella's long dark lashes flutter ever so delicately as she said this?

"It had nothing, I daresay, to do with the idea that Peter proposed to you and you turned him down because his prospects were so poor?" Gervais drawled languidly, at his most wicked.

To her credit, a deep rosy flush colored Annabella's face, and she looked away from her cousin. "Of course not! Why, Peter and I have always considered ourselves engaged. If Uncle Robert had not cut up so badly about the match—and I did not need to have my Season in London—we would have been married by now."

"Now that you will be Lady Marchman to Peter's Lord Marchman," Gervais said coolly, examining his nails. "Your throw, I believe, my dear cousin."

"Well, certainly, now that Peter has come into the title, it changes a great deal," Annabella admitted, picking up the dice box and looking down at the backgammon board.

"Perhaps Peter has changed a great deal in three years," Gervais suggested innocently. "Being held captive in America can hardly be considered salubrious, you know."

"I don't see that it should change anything at all," Annabella said with the supreme confidence of a very spoiled beauty.

Gervais sighed, shaking his head as much as he could between his high starched collar points, watching Annabella laying down her counters. "Well, we shall see what we shall see. But personally, cousin dearest, I think, were I you, I would not count my chickens before they were hatched."

"Pooh," said Annabella, shaking her blond curls.

From her chaise, Mrs. Marchman sighed, popping a comfit into her mouth and wondering if she were about to have one of her spasms. So preoccupied was she with her imaginary complaints, which had served as an excellent buffer between herself and her unpleasant brother-in-law for many years, that she paid very little heed to the dialogue between her nephew and her daughter. Had she been paying attention, she would very properly have objected to Annabella's line of discourse, so perhaps it was just as well, since remonstrating with her willful daughter was precisely the same as trying to control a force of nature, and just as exhausting.

"I shall be glad," she said suddenly, "when Peter opens Marchman House again, and we may all go to London, for I truly do mistrust Dr. Ellicot's opinions of my condition. I need to see Dr. Bailie, so understanding of one's every need."

"Dr. Ellicot is a very capable gentleman," Annabella said absently. "And his prescription that you take fewer quack nostrums and practice a sensible diet and exercise is an excellent idea. Dr. Bailie, however fashionable he might be, simply indulges you. And at two guineas the visit, it is not to be wondered at, Mama."

"How could you, in the bloom of radiant health, understand the suffering of a wretched invalid like me?" moaned Mrs. Marchman, holding a handkerchief beneath her nose.

"Dear me, Aunt Theresa, shall I call for your abigail?" Gervais asked, not without sympathy.

"Dear Gervais, so understanding," Mrs. Marchman almost cooed, smiling feebly at her nephew. "But I am determined to await Peter's return. His letter said it would be today, and what is left of the family must be here to welcome him!"

"As you wish," Gervais murmured with a little bow.

"And speaking of the family," Annabella said wickedly, "we are only fortunate that Great-aunt Aurelia never stirs out of Upper Mount Street, or doubtless we should have her here too, disapproving of us all!"

"Annabella! What a dreadful thing to say," Mrs. Marchman exclaimed.

"I'll wager you'd never say it to Great-aunt's face," Gervais said wickedly. "She quite makes me shake in my boots."

"Oh, pooh," Annabella retorted. "You are quite unafraid of her and she likes you for it. As for me, I am terrified of her, and would as soon face all the lions at Astley's Ampitheater than spend five minutes in her company." She shuddered quite prettily. "The last time I saw Great-aunt, she called me a silly, vain, empty-headed little fool. Can you imagine?"

Gervais smiled. "Aunt Aurelia always says precisely what is on her mind, you know. Your roll, cousin!"

"Well, she will never come out in this weather, that is for certain. That dreadful old coachman of hers would not let her, so at least we are spared that much," Mrs. Marchman said, dosing herself with a spoonful of Jenning's Physick Potion.

"If Peter does not arrive in time for tea, Cook will be having kittens," Annabella observed. "She has made scones in his honor, I am given to understand."

"Peter always was a prime favorite with the servants," Gervais observed lazily. If the truth were to be told, his nerves were a little on edge. Nothing short of an excuse to visit with his lovely cousin would have dragged him away from London at the beginning of what promised to be a most glorious Season. A man who liked his creature comforts could hardly be happy at Marchman Place, where one was not only buried deep in the

West Country, but buried deep in the West Country in a crumbling old pile where mildew permeated everything, the windows in his bedroom rattled with the drafts, the chimneys smoked, and owing to the circumstance of his late uncle having quarreled with the neighbors, there was no company but that of his cousin and his aunt. Nor could he be assured that he would sit down to a good dinner, for Uncle Robert had been notoriously parsimonious, and Gervais was fairly certain that Mrs. Marchman had not taken it upon herself to change the customs of the years. There would be a saddle of mutton, and two removes, with perhaps a curry and a syllabub with the sweet. No wonder poor Annabella wore such an air of discontent, poor child! She hardly needed to be buried in this crumbling misery in half-mourning when she should have been in London, dancing through a pair of slippers every night at Almack's. It was a great deal too bad, and Gervais would very much have liked to remedy that manner of things, but as long as Annabella had taken the notion into her head that what had been between herself and Peter three years ago constituted an engagement, there was very little he could do. Of course he knew that Annabella was thoroughly spoiled, selfish, and totally willful; Gervais was no fool, for all of his fashionable ways. But he also knew that he could provide her with precisely the sort of life she wanted and needed, that of a fashionable London matron. It only remained to be seen if Annabella would come to realize the same.

In the meantime, Gervais was far too composed a gentleman to wear his heart on his sleeve; he was content to wait and see what transpired with Peter's return as the new Lord Marchman.

He did not have long to wait.

The muffled sound of horse's hooves was heard in the drive, and Annabella, with a little exclamation, nearly knocked the gaming table over in her haste to press her face to the streaming window. "Oh, there is a post chaise," she exclaimed, pressing a well-shaped hand against her bosom. "It must be Peter!"

"And about time, too," Gervais muttered, looking at his watch.

"Oh! Oh," Mrs. Marchman said, rather ineffectually attempting to sit upright only to find herself tangled in shawls and cushions, her turban slightly askew. She pressed one plump hand, adorned with several mourning rings, against an equally plump bosom and sought to free herself from her various encumbrances.

"Well, now we shall see," Gervais said languidly, "precisely how our Peter has been affected by his American captivity."

"I hope he is not very *much* changed," Annabella said, darting to the mirror to make a gesture at her blond ringlets and biting her lips to make them redder.

"No need for that, my dear cousin, you are, as always, perfect," Gervais remarked dryly. "Allow me to assist you, Aunt." Gently, he disentangled Mrs. Marchman from her shawls and cushions and assisted her to rise to her feet.

"Thank you, Gervais," she said weakly, adjusting her black moiré turban with an unsteady hand. "If only one felt that one's constitution were stronger . . ." She grasped her fan rather futilely. "The slightest excitement . . . so detrimental to one's constitution . . ."

At that moment, Fishguard, the ancient butler,

opened the doors. Only by the shade of his countenance, which was of a grayish hue, did he betray his emotions as he announced in funereal tones, "Lord and Lady Marchman, madam."

"I feel distinctly faint, Gervais," Mrs. Marchman said in wobbling tones.

7

Perhaps both Annabella and Gervais thought that they had misread Fishguard's announcement. Since the installation of his new wooden teeth, the elderly servitor was not as distinct as he once had been, after all.

Indeed, Annabella was across the room, throwing herself into Peter's arms with a glad if somewhat melodramatic cry before she noticed the woman standing behind him in a cardinal and what she could only castigate as a quiz of a hat.

"Oh, Peter!" she had cried before she saw Sally and had drawn back a step or two, her lovely face a study in puzzlement.

"Hello, Annabella," Peter said, grinning at her. "Still beautiful, little cousin! Aunt Theresa, I see I find you well. Gervais!"

"Indeed," drawled that gentleman, a small, odd smile playing about his face, "I was just wondering how your captivity in America had changed you, Peter. I see that you are very browned by the sun and—" His eyes swept over Sally in such a way that she raised her chin slightly, looking back at him with a long, cool stare.

Well done, whoever you are, Gervais thought. But he did not have long to wait to discover, for Peter had grasped Sally's hand and brought her forward. "This," he said triumphantly, "is the result of what Gervais calls my American captivity. Lady Marchman, formerly Miss Sarah Goldsborough of Santimoke, may I present my aunt, Mrs. Theresa Marchman, my cousin Miss Annabella Marchman, and my other cousin, Mr. Gervais Fallon. My family—my bride. My bride, my family."

"Oh," Mrs. Marchman said, sinking into a chair. "My vinaigrette—" She waved her fan in the air before her face.

But Annabella stood rooted to the spot as if she had been hypnotized, two bright red spots of color appearing in her cheeks, her blue eyes wide as she gazed numbly upon Sally.

For her part, the new Lady Marchman, having undertaken a three-month sea voyage, endured a week of damp English inns and jouncing carriages through the rainy countryside, to arrive at her husband's home only to find it an ancient and decrepit stone pile, sorely in need of repairs and populated by persons who appeared less than ecstatic by her arrival, was, in spite of her natural poise, somewhat intimidated.

The hand she had thrust out, gloved very properly in tan kid, was not taken by Annabella, nor her mother, both of whom seemed to be surveying her as if she had descended upon them from another planet. Even less appealing to her was the tall and fashionable gentleman who was lifting his quizzing glass to one eye, surveying her from the tip of her jean boots to the top of her bombazine bonnet with a slight, almost mocking smile on his lips.

"My dear Lady Marchman," this person said quickly, making a stride across the room to seize her hand and bend low over it in a most elegant gesture, "or perhaps I might call you cousin, since we find ourselves suddenly related?"

"Before our marriage, my wife was Miss Sarah Goldsborough," Lord Marchman told Gervais rather stiffly, putting his hand upon Sally's shoulder.

"Goldsborough," Theresa Marchman repeated vaguely.

"You are an American, then, Cousin Sarah?" Gervais asked politely. Unexpected, as a ray of sunshine emerging from rain clouds, a small smile reached his eyes.

Sally brought her chin up slightly.

"I am a Goldsborough of Water Garden," she said in a firm voice.

"You must excuse us," Theresa Marchman said in a faltering voice, "this is all so—so unexpected."

"Indeed," Annabella murmured, twisting a fringe through her fingers.

"Most unexpected. Peter, why did you not inform us of this—development?"

Peter frowned uneasily, looking at the faces of his relations. Gervais' small smile only served to annoy him further. He shrugged. "Frankly, it did not occur to me that there was any necessity to inform the family. Circumstances were such that communication was difficult, when not impossible. You must know that it was two years before I understood that I had come into the title. It was, as I am certain you can imagine, something of a shock to me."

"Indeed," Gervais said, flicking an imaginary piece of lint from the sleeve of his impeccable coat.

"Indeed," Peter repeated, giving his cousin a lowering look. "Had I not come into it, I believe I might have spared us all and stayed on in America."

"Stayed on in America," Annabella said slowly, twisting the fringes of her shawl through her fingers.

"And why not? It's the land of opportunity for a poor relation with no prospects in England. Certainly no one here would have missed me." His tone was dry, and Sally threw him an odd look, but held her peace, finally aware of the tension in the room, although uncertain of its causes.

Peter had not spoken much of his family.

"Certainly not much for a cadet Marchman to do, eh?" Gervais said slowly.

"Lord Marchman now," Peter said cheerfully enough, but there was still that edge in his voice that Sally had never heard before. "I suppose you would have much liked it, Gervais, my boy, if I were to have stayed put in America and never come back."

"I have no desire to inherit this crumbling pile," Gervais said rather stiffly. "It would cost a fortune to restore it."

"No, Uncle Richard preferred to run his money into gaming hells and loose speculations," Peter agreed thoughtfully, regarding his cousin. "And there's the question of the land. The tenants' cottages are doubtless little more than hovels, and God himself can only tell what the home farms and the fields have gone to."

"I am sure that I would know nothing of that. Farming has fortunately never been one of my interests," Gervais said, barely hiding a yawn. "I take it, my dear Lady Marchman, that it is one of yours?"

Sally suppressed a start. "I was brought up on

a plantation of some eighteen hundred acres, so I am prepared to be of whatever assistance I might to my husband," she said softly.

Peter placed a hand over hers and smiled. "My Sally is pluck to the backbone! Wait until you see her on a horse, or driving to an inch," he declared proudly.

Annabella cast a look over Sally's outmoded American dress—a plain, round muslin affair long out of fashion in England—and allowed herself a quiver of contempt. Whatever, she wondered, could have possessed Peter to chose this rustic booby for his wife? It was beyond all thinking! She could never, ever accept this female as Lady Marchman, to see her take her place at Peter's side, to wear the coronet of a baroness that should have been hers.

A bubble of anger rose in her heart, and Annabella, who had never been deprived of anything she wanted before in her life, especially a man, immediately decided to take what revenge she could against Sally for usurping a man and a position that should have been her own.

We'll see how pluck to the backbone this provincial little booby is, Annabella thought wickedly.

At that moment, the funereal Fishguard appeared in the doorway, bearing a rather tarnished service. Like so many other things at Marchman Place, it had seen better days.

Quite properly, he placed the tray before the new Lady Marchman, and with a bow withdrew to regale his peers belowstairs with his opinion concerning the reaction of the family to the American Lady Marchman.

For a second, there was silence, and then Aunt Theresa sighed loudly. "I see that I shall no longer be considered mistress of Marchman Place

by my own servants," she gusted in die-away
accents, giving Sally a frigid and rather fish-eyed
stare.

"If you have been accustomed to pour, then I
would think it best that you should continue to
do so," Sally said quickly. "After all, it will take
me some time to accustom myself to my duties
here, and I shall depend upon you and Annabella
to tell me how I must go on."

"Oh, you can depend upon them, I assure you,"
Peter said cheerfully, taking the tray and placing
it before his offended aunt. "Aunt Theresa and
Annabella have lived here forever, you know. I
am sure that they will do everything in their
power to make you feel comfortable and at ease."

"I'm sure," Gervais murmured darkly. "Won't
you, Annabella?"

"Oh, of course," she replied thickly. "It is simply that it is such a shock, Sally—if I may be so
bold as to call you Sally—since we find ourselves
so close related?"

"Of course you may. Let us not stand too formal," Sally replied, accepting a cup of tea from
Aunt Theresa's disdainful hands.

"You must tell us how you and Peter chanced
to meet," Annabella added. "I am certain that it
is a most interesting story."

"I met her in jail," Peter said cheerfully, putting his arm about Sally and giving her a good-
natured hug.

It was a small miracle that the china teapot
did not fall from Mrs. Marchman's trembling
hands. "In jail, did you say, Peter?" she asked in
faltering accents.

"Yes. She was rather the cause of having me
incarcerated there, you see. She coshed me with
an Imari vase."

"C-coshed you with a what?" Aunt Theresa demanded, clutching her bosom.

"I believe that Peter means Lady Marchman smashed an Imari vase over his head," Gervais put in. Evidently despairing of ever receiving his tea, he had gotten up to prepare it himself. "And what, pray tell, Peter, had you done to deserve to be coshed by an Imari vase?" he asked, his voice droll.

Peter laughed. "I was stealing food from her father's house. She was pluck to the backbone. She came into the dining room and saw me stuffing ham into my pockets and picked up the vase and—*whoosh!* Down I went!"

Annabella shuddered. "I should have fainted," she said primly, as if this were the proper reaction to be expected of a young lady in such circumstances.

"But Sally didn't! She thought about it first. I was ashore as a part of a raiding party, and was where I was not supposed to be. She's a game one."

"Indeed," Gervais said slowly.

Sally had not looked up from her teacup. She noticed the edge of the saucer was sadly chipped and that there was a draft from the window directly behind her. "It seemed," she announced after a beat, "to be quite appropriate, under the circumstances. Afterward, of course, I felt very sorry for Peter and took a basket of food to the county jail, where they were keeping him. The war did not really reach our part of the country, you see, and everyone was at a loss as to what might be done with him."

"They were going to hang me," Peter announced.

"A great deal too bad that they did not," Gervais retorted, crossing one leg over the other and settling back in his chair, his eyes glittering wickedly.

"Wasn't it just?" Peter agreed flatly, meeting his cousin's eyes. "Instead, Colonel Goldsborough—Sally's father—paroled me, and so we began our courtship."

"I see," Mrs. Marchman murmured disapprovingly. "How very fortunate for Lady Marchman."

"No, I am the fortunate one. When Sally discovered that I was a peer, she was not at all certain that she wanted to marry me, you see."

"Americans must have the quaintest ideas," Annabella purred. "You must tell me, dear, where you found that bonnet. I had one just like it, five or six years ago."

Two faint spots of color appeared in Sally's cheeks, and she gave Annabella a flat stare that said nothing. "We have taken all our fashions from Paris, of course," she said eventually.

"Well, Sally hasn't had much time to put together a trousseau. We were married, and then two days later we caught a ship from Baltimore to Portsmouth. But when I open Marchman House, I'm depending on you, Annabella, to show her what she shall need to be Lady Marchman."

"Oh, I shall be glad to do that," Annabella said, and Gervais cast her a sideways glance, the set of his lips not quite pleasant.

"How—how very interesting," Mrs. Marchman faltered amid the teacups. "Doubtless you have a great many other plans in store for us, Peter?"

Peter frowned, looking about the room. "It would seem to me, Aunt, that the first thing to be done is to try to pull the estate back into some semblance of order. Tomorrow, I'll want to see the bailiff—is it still old Caper? Good. Everything is crying out to be redone, replaced, or repaired. But I daresay that Sally can take care of the house, do it up to suit her tastes, if she likes. It'll be a job of work to undo twenty years' neglect, but I'm the man who will accomplish it, now that I'm master here."

Sally looked about her, wondering at the job that Peter had given her. The upholstery and the drapes were as near to being in rags as made no differences, and the walls cried out for paint, peeling and chipped as they were.

"Change Marchman Place?" Annabella cried, pressing her hands to her heart. "But everything is just as it was, ever. For centuries! You cannot just sweep in and change history."

"You can, however, repair a drafty window and replace a rent curtain," Sally said quietly, her voice determined.

"Just so," Peter said firmly, biting into a scone. "And now that Sally is mistress here, I'm sure that she'll make this old place shine again, inside and out."

"Oh, I am sure," Gervais said.

"I feel distinctly faint. Annabella, please, support me to my room," Mrs. Marchman said.

"Of course, Mama," the beauty agreed, assisting the older woman to wobble uncertainly toward the doors.

"Well, Peter, my lad," Gervais said when they had gone. "As always, you have managed to set everything to sixes and sevens."

"Yes," Peter replied, his mouth full, "I was always rather good at that, wasn't I?" He smiled at Sally. "Well, my love, there you have my family. I'm sure you'll come to like them by and by."

Sally inclined her head and looked at him.

8

Shortly before dinner, Mr. Fallon, correct to a turn in knee breeches and a pearl-gray waistcoat, left the capable hands of his valet and descended the stairs to the green salon, pausing only for a moment to assure himself that all was well by his reflection in the long glass in the hall.

He was by no means surprised to find his cousin Annabella in that drafty chamber, seated beside the fire and looking even more ravishing than usual in a dinner dress of dove-wing silk, banded about the hem with ruches of lace and corsaged with white satin ribbons.

"Blue-deviled, my dear coz?" Gervais inquired with deceptive casualness, gracefully seating himself opposite her.

Annabella lifted a pink and white countenance to look at her cousin. Her enormous blue eyes were swimming. "How could he?" she demanded in wounded tones.

Gervais shrugged. "How could he not, after all? Only consider, Annabella, that you had rejected him."

There was a great deal of truth in what Gervais said, but Annabella, whose mind was not noted for logical progressions, merely shook her blond curls. "I only meant to hurt him a little," she said, twisting the strings of her reticule about in her fingers. "I was only teasing him."

"Teasing him enough to send him away into the navy in a pet," Gervais reminded her. "You told him, as I recall, that his future was not good enough to suit you."

"Well, it was not at the time. Robert stood to inherit, and one had so many beaux in London that one did not know where to turn—" This somewhat disingenuous speech only caused her cousin to lean back in his chair and smile, shaking his head. "If you hadn't been closeted off here in Devon in mourning for Uncle Richard and Robert, coz, I daresay you would have married yourself off very well to one of those London beaux, and have become a fashionable matron by now."

Her sentimental self-portrait totally destroyed by Gervais' comment, Annabella looked at him wrathfully. "How can you be so—so insensible?" she demanded.

Gervais, flicking an imaginary piece of lint from his lapel, gave his cousin a lazy smile from beneath his eyelids, shaking his head slightly as he did so. "You, my dear cousin, have made me a cynic. Your constant rejection of my suit, your heartless treatment of one who cherishes the deepest feelings toward you—"

"Oh, stop, Gervais, do," Annabella said rather testily. "You know that you don't care a pea for me."

"I, *au contraire*, know nothing of the sort," Gervais said lazily.

"And her! Good God, have you ever seen anything less eligible to become Lady Marchman? That hair, and *freckles!*" Annabella exclaimed bitterly. "I ask you. And that accent. Wholly

inappropriate! She speaks as if she had a mouthful of molasses, and perhaps she does. And those
clothes! Good God, did you ever see anything so
dowdy as that cardinal? Why, I daresay, even my
maid no longer wears a cardinal. And the way in
which she dresses her hair! Was there ever anyone more provincial? I daresay she will eat with
her knife."

"Oh, I don't know," Gervais replied slowly,
examining his fingernails. "For my part, I think
Miss Sarah admirably suited to our Peter."

"To think," said a voice in the accents of high
tragedy, "that I should hear such things in my
house, from the nephew upon whom I wholly
depended," Mrs. Marchman said as she entered
the room.

"Come now, Aunt Theresa, not you, too," Gervais said bracingly as he rose to escort his aunt to
her chaise, where she reclined, amid many shawls,
with a long-suffering sigh.

"It is all that one can do to accept Peter's
bride—" Mrs. Marchman shuddered eloquently—
"with at least the outward semblance of complai-
sance. But every sensibility is offended. An
American! Is this what the Marchmans have come
to? Only think of what the neighbors shall say.
Of what society shall say." Quite overcome, Mrs.
Marchman sank back into the cushions and had
recourse to Bailey's Powders before she was at
least partially restored. "Every sensibility is offended," she repeated woefully.

"If I were you, I wouldn't care what the neighbors say," Gervais drawled. "Since Uncle Richard managed to quarrel with almost everyone
about, about almost everything, none of the neighbors have set foot near Marchman Place since
his funeral, to my knowledge. And then I think

only half of them came to be certain he was dead."

"What a terrible thing to say," Mrs. Marchman gasped.

"Well, it is true," Annabella said bitterly. "For more than two years, no parties, no dances, no balls, no gay clothes! It has been more than a person can stand, when one yearns to be gay rather than buried in the country in this way." Looking rather petulant, she added. "And now, when they come, it will be to meet her! We shall be quite laughed out of the county."

"Every sensibility is offended," Mrs. Marchman repeated again, looking very much as if she wished to go off into a swoon. "But at least now that Peter has returned, we may be able to put off mourning and go back into colors, and for that, I shall be grateful. Perhaps he will even open Marchman House again."

"Yes, then we may be laughed at by all of London. Can you see that American hostessing a ball at Marchman House? A London ball?"

"I would imagine that she will acquit herself upon every score. There is nothing featherbrained about the new Lady Marchman," Gervais said. "Indeed, I have decided to take a liking for her."

"Odious beast!" Annabella exclaimed. "How could you, when you can clearly see how her presence has overthrown Mama and me?"

Although Gervais might have said that Mrs. Marchman was possessed of an ample-enough jointure of her own to set up her own establishment, he did not do so, instead contenting himself with a small, tight smile. "Perhaps I shall contrive to bring her into fashion."

"You would not dare," Annabella said. "Oh, Gervais, you would not dare. I should be furious!"

"Should you, my dear cousin?" he asked blithely. "Then that would be all the more reason why I should wish to do it."

"Peter despises society," Mrs. Marchman said smugly. "So that should put an end upon that, for he will never allow her to go to London."

"We know nothing of that," Annabella said bitterly. "Doubtless, he shall ask you to present her at court."

Mrs. Marchman was only capable of emitting a low moan at the very thought. "My health would never stand such a thing," she announced in tones of satisfaction.

Since Gervais held the opinion that his aunt's constitution was far more robust than she allowed, he said nothing immediately, but inspected his white stockings. "Perhaps Great-aunt Aurelia can be convinced to bring her out, then."

This was greeted with incredulous stares from both his aunt and his cousin. "Great-aunt Aurelia! Surely not! You know what a stickler she is," Annabella exclaimed. "Only think, if we are shocked, how she will feel about all of this!"

"All of what?" Peter Marchman, correctly if not as splendidly attired as his cousin Gervais, appeared in the doorway, looking his relations over with mild blue eyes.

"I fear your unexpected arrival with a new bride has profoundly shocked the family," Gervais said easily. "But not half so much as that cravat is shocking me. Tell me, dear boy, have you picked up your appalling sartorial tastes from your stint in the navy or your American captivity?"

"Hang yourself, Gervais, lad," Peter said easily, long accustomed to the barbs of his sartorially resplendent cousin. "We all can't cut the counter coxcomb in quite the way *you* do!"

"Thank the Lord for small favors," Gervais retorted, in no way discomfited by Peter's retaliation.

For his part, Peter clasped his hands behind his back and made his way toward the fire, from which vantage point he surveyed his family from placid blue eyes, little suspecting the storm he had raised in Marchman Place by his unexpected arrival with a new and alien bride. "It is shocking how much Uncle Richard allowed the house to run to ground," he said, frowning slightly. "I have no doubt that the estates are in even worse management than they were when I left."

"I would have no idea," Mrs. Marchman said. "The bailiff has always managed such affairs, you know."

"Yes, and I do for all of that," Peter said. "Tomorrow, first thing, I intend to send for Caper and go through accounts with him." Peter shook his head. "Believe me, I never thought to inherit, but now that I have, it seems best to me to make myself acquainted with all facets of this."

"You could start by having that loose board in my room nailed down," Annabella said. "Heaven knows, Thomas has never obliged me by doing so, and Uncle Richard never cared a scrap for anything but his own comfort, so why should he?"

"There's more than a loose board that needs to be repaired in this place," Peter said as a burst of smoke puffed up from the chimney. "One would hardly know where to start to make all the repairs that are necessary here. The roof leaks, Fishguard tells me that the subcellars flood in the spring, and I should not wonder but what the casements go back to the Conquest.''

"Hardly that far, old man," Gervais observed, "but close enough nonetheless. My room is so drafty that I dare not close my eyes all night for the rattling of the panes. You have your work cut out for you, Peter, and frankly, I would not stand in your shoes for all the baronies in England."

"No, you are the lucky one, Gervais," Peter said, looking at his cousin narrowly. "This is certainly not what I had bargained for, in and all. I was never put in the way of knowing exactly how things stood, but now I begin to get a very good idea. Uncle Richard wrung every groat he could from the estates, and put not a penny back into them. He squandered what there was at the gaming tables and never gave a thought for anyone but himself. And Robert, I fear would not have been much better. I barely know where I should start."

"Indeed, my boy, yours will be an uphill job," Gervais remarked complacently.

"I am quite sorry to be so tardy, but I lost my way in some of the passageways," Sally said as she came through the door, meeting two feminine and hostile pairs of eyes with a level brown-eyed stare of her own.

"There you are, my darling," Peter said, coming forward to greet her, taking her hand. "I'm sorry! I should have thought to send Fishguard up to escort you down."

Sally shrugged lightly. "It is not of the least consequence," she said. She was dressed in a pale-yellow silk dinner dress with capped sleeves and an embroidered hem. Not precisely in the first stare of European fashion, Gervais thought lazily, but quite becoming and without the least impropriety for dinner in the country. Point to you, Lady Marchman!

"I suppose if one is not used to these hallways, one can become lost. I daresay your home in America is in no way as large as Marchman Place, Sarah?" Annabella said, raising an eyebrow suggestively.

"No way as large, and by far more comfortable, elegant, and modern," Peter answered for his wife. "Indeed, I think that I shall consider Water Garden when I come to make my improvements here."

"But, Peter, this is a wonderful old place," Sally said, draping her India shawl about her shoulders as a draft hit her full blast from the casements.

"I suppose that you will want to make all sorts of modern improvements, Sarah?" Mrs. Marchman demanded from her cushions. "Changing all the old traditions and customs of the place?"

"I have not had much time to give it any thought," Sally said carefully, looking at Mrs. Marchman as if she were one of the things she would like to improve upon. "I shall have to do as Peter wishes, of course."

"But you are Lady Marchman now," Annabella exclaimed in silky tones. "It will be up to you to redecorate the house."

At that moment, Fishguard opened the doors. "Dinner is served, my lady," he intoned, looking meaningfully at Sarah.

"Yes, of course," she said, far more easily than she was feeling. "Shall we all? I confess that I am starving."

Annabella, who would have endured having her fingernails ripped out before she would have admitted in the presence of men that she was in need of anything so mundane as earthly sustenance, narrowed her eyes as she looked toward Sarah, and caught her tongue between her teeth.

As if he had sensed her thoughts, Gervais was at her elbow at once, murmuring that he would escort her to the dining room.

Peter, having assisted his aunt to rise to her feet and select whatever nostrums and powders she could not sit down to dinner without having in her possession, provided the complaining woman with escort, leaving Sarah to trail in their wake.

Ever since she had discovered the true circumstances of Peter's birthright, Sally had been uneasy. But now that she had confronted his family, face to face, she was positively ready to turn and run.

It was abundantly clear to her that these strangers considered her presence alien and an affront. Doubtless, this haughty blond beauty and her ailing mama had lived a great part of their lives in Marchman Place, and doubtless feared that a new bride would wreak changes into their ordered lives. Being a member of a large and varied family herself, Sarah quickly decided that her best course would be to win them over slowly. She was well conscious that they were Peter's family, after all, and therefore, in some fashion sacrosanct. She had only to imagine any of her many brothers arriving upon the doorstep with an unknown wife to understand their feelings.

But still, she could not suppress her feelings of alienation and that sense of aloneness which may derive from finding oneself in a strange country, among strangers.

But she would not have been Sarah Goldsborough of Water Garden, daughter of the colonel, had she not squared her shoulders and raised her chin as she was placed in her seat at the head of the table; a position yielded to her precedence, it would seem, only by the greatest reluctance of Mrs. Marchman, who had been, until that afternoon, mistress of Marchman Place.

Nonetheless, Sally was determined that here, at least, she would claim her place, for to do less would have reflected badly upon Peter.

She was not displeased to find Peter's rather droll cousin Gervais had been seated to her right, although, of necessity, the table was uneven, Annabella having been placed at her left, where she was bending her blond head very close to Peter's dark curls, talking of heaven knew what.

As Fishguard, on felt-slippered feet, brought in the first course of a turbot poached in wine sauce, Gervais picked up his glass and smiled over the rim at Sally.

"I daresay you must find all of this a bit dismaying, ma'am. I know that I should, were I in your shoes." He gestured about the room, which in even the half-light of the candelabrum, betrayed the same woeful neglect as the rest of the house. The heavy velvet drapes hung to the windows were practically shredded with age, and the wallpaper so ancient as to be nearly blackened, particularly above the fireplace, which, like every other hearth in Marchman Place, smoked with depressing regularity. The very board at which they sat was deeply scratched and worn, so much so that even beneath the carefully darned covers, Sally could see the marks of meals taken by persons long passed on.

"Yes, I suppose that it does need a bit of work," Sally admitted carefully, "but I would hesitate to instigate too many changes until I knew precisely where I stood, you know."

Gervais gave her a sharp look, much different from his usual carefully controlled air of languor of fashion. "I think, my lady, that you will do," he said at last.

"Will I?" Sarah asked coolly. She cut a tiny piece of turbot with the edge of a rather tarnished fork. "The question is, do I want to?"

Gervais laughed. "Stabble me, my lady. 'Give me, I know you are not conversant with London cant, most improper, but what I mean to say is, yes, point and counterpoint well taken! And this ain't the worst of the family, either. You should only have had to seen Uncle Richard and Cousin Robert in *their* time! Loose fish, the pair of them, and never a thought for anyone's pleasure but their own. So, I understand it is with all who are hunting mad. But every cent they ever had between the pair of them went into the stables, or down in the pasteboards, or off into some other mad scheme. Dashed ramshackle pair. But then, all of Prinny's cronies are ramshackle, I suppose. Movin' about with the Prince Regent just ain't done, you know."

In spite of herself, Sally felt her lips twitching. "No, I did not know. But I am glad that you have enlightened me upon the point, for I was quite set upon meeting him."

"I say," Gervais exclaimed, much shocked, and then, catching the glitter in Sally's eye, relaxed perceptibly. "Glad you don't mean that, because I have a strong feeling you wouldn't like it if you did."

"I have a strong feeling you are quite correct," Sally replied calmly. "But you must tell me more about, er, Uncle Richard and Cousin Robert, if you please!"

Gervais toyed with his fork. "Well, there you have it! Care-for-nobodies, the pair of them! All the Marchmans are like that, you see. Or you will see! Matter of fact, ma'am, I'd step lightly, were I you, until I saw just how things stood."

"Mmmm," Sally said, lifting her wineglass to her lips. "And pray tell me, Cousin Gervais, how do things stand?"

"Knee-deep in blood, dear ma'am! Peter was always the black sheep of the family, you see."

"Ah?" Sarah's eyebrows lifted slightly.

"Indeed," Gervais responded. "Well, not precisely what you're thinking. Always a game 'un, our Peter, and up to every rig and row in town, what's more. There, that's rare praise for me, you know, for Peter and I never did manage to scrape together without pulling hair since we were boys. But he was orphaned early on, and came to live at Marchman Place with Uncle Richard, and he and Cousin Robert were wont to plot all sorts of distasteful mischief against me. Something I can never forgive them for, even now," Gervais added, dabbing at his lips with a linen napkin. "Rowdies, they were, proper rowdies! Then, of course, Uncle Fredrick managed to stick *his* spoon into the wall, and Aunt Theresa and Annabella came to live at Marchman Place. Uncle Fred, you understand, being as neck or nothing as Robert and Uncle Richard, came a cropper in the field. His horse cleared a fence, but he didn't. So, there you have the family—or what's left of it, save for Great-aunt Aurelia, and her you don't even want to know. She lives in London, on Upper Mount Street, with a great number of pug dogs, and so terrifying is she that even

I am terrified of her! And I assure you, cousin, very little terrifies me! She was a great arbiter of society in her day, and devilish high in the instep. Doesn't like Americans."

"She would seem not to be the only one who feels that way," Sally said in a low voice, looking about the table.

Gervais shrugged. He considered whether or not he ought to apprise Lady Marchman of the situation between her husband and Annabella, and decided against it.

"Quite natural that Aunt Theresa and Annabella should be up in the boughs. This is their home, you know, and doubtless they're afraid of the changes you will make."

"Doubtless," Sally sad dryly. "But I cannot understand why a woman as lovely as Annabella has not married yet."

"Her Season was cut short by Uncle Richard's death. Mourning and half-mourning, you know! Oh, she was top-of-the-trees. All the fellows wanted a turn with Annabella, and doubtless she would have buckled herself by the end of the Season to some duke or another, if Uncle Richard hadn't been so selfish as to drown in the middle of it," Gervais said lightly.

If Sarah was shocked by his irreverent attitude, she gave no sign, but rather smiled faintly. "And there was no other reason?" she asked.

"I wouldn't know," Gervais lied calmly.

"I see," Sally said thoughtfully.

There was no more conversation as Fishguard was removing the turbot, to replace it with a dressed chicken in lobster sauce. Dutifully, Sarah turned her conversation to her husband's aunt.

Mrs. Marchman, however, proved to be a daunting conversationalist, as she was far more interested in addressing her chicken than her new niece. For an invalid, Sarah thought, she was certainly possessed of an excellent appetite. As an aunt, however, she could not help but feel Mrs. Marchman left something to be desired.

Attempts to catch the eye of her husband were unavailing. Annabella seemed to have enraptured him at the head of the table, and the two of them were talking in low voices, their heads placed very close together, and their conversation punctuated only by bursts of laughter.

If Sarah felt a sense of discomfort, she gave no indication of it, but merely picked at her chicken. Like the turbot before it, it was sadly overdone, and almost at the point of turning. She began to hold no very high opinion of the chef and resolved that she must speak to the staff at the first opportunity.

After dinner, the ladies withdrew to the green salon, leaving Gervais and Peter to their port and cigarillos. Mrs. Marchman immediately took to her chaise, where she spent a great deal of time playing among her bottles and tins, selecting just what she thought would relieve her dyspepsia with as much pleasure as another woman would have selected a dress.

All but ignoring Sarah, Annabella drifted toward the pianoforte, where she proceeded to play—rather badly, to Sarah's mind—a series of singularly depressing and maudlin ballads concerning lost loves, blighted hopes, and suicide pacts between forbidden lovers.

Seating herself gingerly in a wing chair beside the fire, Sarah repressed a twinge of homesickness and rather abstractedly perused a very back issue of *The Gentleman's Magazine*.

She was following the exploits of Tom and

Jerry, two Corinthians out on the town, with mild interest when Peter and Gervais, both of them glowing with the effects of port, finally joined the ladies.

From there, the evening degenerated into a game of whist between Gervais, Peter, Mrs. Marchman, and Annabella, for chicken stakes. Sarah, who did not play whist, yawned beside the fire until the tea tray was brought in.

Mrs. Marchman made, to Sarah's mind, an elaborate martyrdom of relinquishing the privilege of pouring tea to Lady Marchman, and Annabella declined, with a morbid sigh, to partake of the cucumber cakes.

Sarah, having let down her hair and arraying herself in her nightgown and an embroidered dressing gown of peacock blue, passed between the connecting doors that joined her room with that of her husband and sat down upon the feather mattress of an ancient Tudor bedstead. She watched Peter neatly lay out his things upon the top of his bureau and surveyed the surroundings distastefully.

Neither chamber was in what Sarah would have called good shape. Her room, done up in a particularly vile shade of rose damask, had a shredding carpet and an ornate marble fireplace that had been chipped in several places.

My lord's bedroom had a faded and particularly nasty French paper depicting rather graphic hunting scenes. Moths had been at both the carpet and the heavy velour draperies hung against the big, drafty casement windows, and it smelled rather depressingly of spirits of turpentine, which someone had ineffectually used to drive away the pests.

"Well," Peter said, looking at Sarah in the mirror, "what do you think?"

Sarah bit her lip to restrain herself from the acid comment that rose to mind, and merely raised a foot and pointed a bare toe at the wall. "It is all very interesting," she said finally.

"Good God, I had no idea of how badly everything has deteriorated, Sally. I never should have dragged you into this mess, had I known."

"I've never shied from an adventure yet, Peter," she replied seriously. "But you are quite right—" As she picked at a handful of the counterpane, the velour shredded through her fingers. "There is much to be done to make this place livable again."

Stripping out of his smalls, Peter walked across the room and lay on the bed beside his wife, putting his arm about her shoulders. "I'll bet that you thought being a lady would be much more church and state than this."

Sally laughed, resting her head on Peter's shoulder. "Indeed, now who's talking American, Mr. Marchman?"

"I am certain that the broad drawl in my speech has quite sunk me below reproach with my family," he said easily. "What do you think of them?"

Sally bit her lip again. "I think Gervais most interesting," she said at last.

"Is not Annabella a stunning beauty?"

Sally glanced him, but his expression was perfectly serious. "Yes, she is most attractive," she replied carefully.

"And my Aunt Theresa is something of a character, with her nostrums and remedies," Peter continued fondly. "I cannot imagine Marchman Place without her."

I can, Sally thought, but said nothing.

"Tomorrow, I must consult with my bailiff and my agent. I shall ask Annabella to show you about the house and introduce you to the staff; she's the one to do it."

"It sounds wonderful," Sally said dryly.

"I thought you would like that," Peter replied, yawning sleepily.

Long after his gentle rhythmic breathing had started up, Sally still lay awake, staring into the darkness, wondering how she was to make do.

9

Annabella, in a high-necked round gown of dove-gray crepe, trimmed with satin ribands, stood at the foot of the grand staircase, eyeing Sally haughtily as she descended in a figured French muslin, cut high beneath the bust and fixed with slashed sleeves and ruched hem.

"You really ought to be in mourning, or at least half-mourning, and so should Peter. I wonder that he did not tell you so," she said coolly. "But I suppose it don't signify, buried as we are here in the country, and very near to putting off our black gloves."

"No, I suppose it to be of very little consequence," Sally returned evenly, giving the beauty a flat stare of her own.

Annabella had the grace of flush. "Very well! I believe you met all the servants yesterday. At any rate Fishguard had them lined up in the hallway, I believe, so we may pass upon that. If you will follow me, please!" She picked up her skirts and passed down the corridor, through a series of rooms. "These are the state apartments, and they are opened generally on public days. You will, of course, note that there is a great deal of armor. It is not, as you might suspect, *dépoque*, but was in fact collected by the first Baron

91

Marchman in Tudor times. I daresay he knew a bargain when he saw it. All the Marchmans do."

Very much in this vein, they proceeded through the series of corridors, each one more in a ramshackle fashion than the last. Everywhere Sally saw gilt dulled with age, brass desperately in need of polish, and damask and velvet shredding to dust with age. Whatever else she might be, it soon became apparent to Sally that Mrs. Marchman was definitely not a housekeeper. In these circumstances, Miss Henrietta would have gone down on her own hands and knees and polished and scrubbed rather than allow things to decay in such a shoddy manner; and to a great extent, Sally, who hated housework but loathed mismanagement even more, had already begun to make mental notes about what she intended to say to Mrs. Gunning, the housekeeper.

Annabella, who had known Marchman Place in no other state than that of neglect, was inclined to look upon the very dust upon the Hepplewhite tables as somehow sacrosanct and inviolate. When Sarah chanced to make some comment, as she ran a finger through the mildew budding on an ancient tapestry fire screen, the beauty's eyes shot upward, and she sighed eloquently.

"Of course, my dear Sarah, you cannot be expected to understand how ancient and how valuable are the traditions of Marchman Place. In your country, I am certain that everything is new, and quite unestablished, whereas here we place a great value upon the past."

"Not enough, I would think, Annabella, to keep it up properly," Sarah said flatly. "I am sure that Peter would agree with me that these rooms have not been cleaned well in a number of years."

"I cannot picture Peter wanting anything about Marchman Place changed," Annabella retorted somewhat dramatically. "After all, this has been his home nearly all of his life. I doubt that you can begin to understand that he places importance upon things remaining just as they are."

"I shall do whatever makes him comfortable," Sally said evenly.

"Just so," Annabella said with the faintest trace of long-suffering in her voice. "And now, we have the picture gallery . . ."

Sarah dutifully gazed upon long-dead Marchmans done up in style by Patrius, Holbein, and Lawrence, but even as Annabella was recounting their various histories, her companion had begun to note that the beauty loved none of this for what it was, but rather for what its value meant to her. As Miss Henrietta was wont to say, Sally thought, Annabella knew the price of everything and the worth of nothing.

It was enlightening as to Annabella's character, and Sarah tucked it away with the strong feeling that there might come a time when she would need just such a weapon.

Annabella was greatly shocked when Sally requested to see both the servants' quarters and the kitchens. Never in her entire life had she ventured into either domain. The thought simply would not have occurred to her, and she was nakedly astonished at the cool way in which Sally interviewed Cook and took stock of the facilities.

Upon encountering an equally astonished Mrs. Gunning upon the stairs, Sarah demanded to be shown the linen boards, the storage rooms, and the wine cellar, and though Mrs. Gunning was as astonished as Annabella by such a request from Lady Marchman, she could not help but allow her respect for Sally to increase considerably, as she later informed Mr. Fishguard.

"American she may be, Amos, and that cannot be denied, but she's well-bred, and what's more, she knows how to hold household, which is more than can be said for Mrs. Theresa Marchman, if you know what I mean."

"Indeed, Mary, I had my trepidations, but it would seem to me that Mr. Peter—that is to say, Lord Marchman—has chosen well. Perhaps between the two of them, we may yet see Marchman Place as it was in the old days."

"That's to be seen," Mrs. Gunning replied carefully. "It's to be hoped that the late lord didn't leave things so dipped in the bucket as to be no way out. Or that Mrs. Theresa and Miss Annabella won't try to fly up in the boughs."

If the reader might suspect that Mrs. Marchman and her daughter were not universally loved belowstairs, she may have surmised correctly. On the other hand, Sally's stock soared, once it was seen that she was a lady who knew what she was about.

They had had their doubts; now they believed that Sally would do.

Annabella and Mrs. Marchman thought otherwise.

"Well," said the beauty as she came into her mother's dressing room just before lunch, "I believe I may have been said to do my duty."

Mrs. Marchman, who was just tying a cap beneath her chin, immediately reached for her vinaigrette, as Annabella, her mouth set into a sullen line that quite ruined her beauty, threw herself into a chair. "Whatever do you mean, my love?" Mrs. Marchman asked carefully.

"I mean, Mama, that I have shown precious

Sarah all over the house. And I do mean all over the house! She wanted to see it from cellars to attic. She even went into the kitchen."

"The kitchen?" Mrs. Marchman asked, much shocked. "Whatever for?"

"To inspect the facilities and talk with Cook! I apprehend that she means to hold household together without further delay. Have you ever heard of anything so outrageous?"

Mrs. Marchman, seeing those duties she had held abhorrent for a number of years slipping away from her, instead of feeling relief, felt only indignation. "Well, of all the encroaching creatures!" she said, waving her vinaigrette beneath her own nose. "Of course, my love, you realize that there is nothing we can do about it. That—that American thing *is* the new Lady Marchman!"

"She is an odious mistake that Peter made when he was imprisoned in that dreadful country! Well, I am not precisely certain that it is a dreadful country, but I would suppose that it were, from all accounts. Oh, Mama, it is above all things insupportable. One could stand to lose him to an Englishwoman, an heiress, perhaps, with a great deal of money to restore Marchman Place to its old glory—but an American! It is above all things insupportable!"

Mrs. Marchman, long used to Annabella's tantrums, made faint, fluttering noises in the back of her throat, and reached for Dr. Trent's Restorative Elixirs, but Annabella, in a passion much like that of a spoiled child who has been thwarted in wanting something, continued on heedlessly.

"Odious, encroaching creature! I should die before I will see her mistress of Marchman Place! It is insupportable, particularly when that role should have been mine. And would have been, had not that creature come."

"Oh, Annabella, do not speak this way. Very soon we shall be out of black gloves, and then, I daresay, you will have your choice of any peer in the land."

"But it is Peter that I want," Annabella said, quite forgetting that she had spurned his advances when he was but Mr. Marchman. "And I mean to have him!"

Mrs. Marchman squawked. "Annabella," she gasped, having recourse to Johnson's Nostrum, Elixir of Health, and Roche's Powder, all at once. "Whatever do you mean?"

"I mean that once it has been shown to Peter how very unsuitable this mésalliance is, he will waste no time in procuring a divorce from the House of Lords—"

"A divorce?" Mrs. Marchman quavered, truly horrified. "My love, think of the scandal!"

"Oh, who should care? Peter made a mistake. He married an American nobody, quite ineligible to become Lady Marchman, repents of his mistake, and seeks redress. I daresay the matter will be dispatched with a great deal of ease."

"Annabella, you cannot be serious."

The beauty's eyes narrowed. "Not serious?" Watch me!" she exclaimed.

"Oh, I feel quite unwell. Certainly, Peter's wife is an insupportable, American creature, but divorce . . . Only consider the scandal should your name become entangled into it."

"I shall take care that it does not," Annabella promised. "And you, Mama, must say no word to anyone! Especially Gervais! It is most exasperating, but he seems to have taken one of his unpredictable likings to that girl. God forbid he should contrive to bring her into fashion," Annabella said with a shudder.

"God forbid that Peter should discover this scheme of yours," Mrs. Marchman said faintly. "He would cast us both out, and then we should have to go and live with your Aunt Aurelia."

"Don't worry," Annabella laughed a little hysterically. "He shall never know what I have plotted. But, after all, it is for his own good."

Still in his riding clothes, Peter came through the side door from the terrace, and into the library, where he found Sally alone, with an apron over her gown of dimity, looking quite domestic as she stood on the ladder and scanned the spines of the books.

Peter grinned and, on silent boots, trod up the carpet behind her, grasping her about the waist and swooping her off her perch in order to bestow a kiss upon her cheek and another on her lips. "My little housewife!" he exclaimed as Sally suppressed an astonished exclamation.

"Oh! It's you!" She managed to say, wrapping her arms about Peter's neck as he kissed the light dusting of freckles across her nose.

"Yes, it is I, as all the very bad villains say in all the worst plays!" Peter laughed, sitting down upon a sofa, from which rose a cloud of dust, with Sally in his lap. "Is this how you elect to spend your days, then? Dusting the books in the library? I thought we employed several housemaids who had that job while they are eating us out of house and home."

"I was curious to see precisely what you have here, dearest," Sally replied. "Some quite amazing volumes, and very old, too."

Peter laughed. "I daresay they are old, at least!

To my knowledge no one at Marchman Place has bought a book in the past two generations. Annabella procures some rather dreadful novels from the lending library in Ottery Saint Mary, but other than that, no Marchman has ever been known to read more than the racing sheets."

"That would explain the sad neglect of this room. I really must speak to Mrs. Gunning about letting things go so much—"

"You may take that as the fault of Aunt Theresa, who is, at best, an indifferent housekeeper. However, now that you are in charge, I shall expect a house that is spotless and well-run, dominated by a domestic martinet."

Sally looked a little dismayed, but Peter merely laughed, kissing her again.

"And how did your day go?" she managed to ask.

Peter sighed, at once serious. "You do not want to know," he said, shaking his head. "Things are at a worse standstill than I had thought. Everything's been let run to rack and ruin, Sally, and gone shockingly bad. The land yields a tenth as much as it did, I am given to understand, when my grandfather was alive. Uncle Richard was careless, to say the least."

"As bad as all of that?"

"Worse. It may take years of careful management to bring everything around again to what it ought to be. You see, I had never been put in the way of learning about these things before, no one expecting Uncle Richard and Cousin Robert to turn as they did; and now, I've got to learn everything from start. And there's precious little money to work with, either."

"Peter, you know that we have my inheritance to work with. A letter to Father, and—"

Peter's face took on a mulish look. "I won't take your money, Sally, my love, so put that idea out of your head at once. The colonel may settle it upon our children, if he wishes, but I won't have it said that I married you for your money."

"As you wish. But, Peter, this is to be *my* home now, also, and it would seem only logical to me that I should invest my capital where it would do the most good. And Father would agree."

Peter shook his head. "I know that your heart is in the right place, Sally, but that's just not the way things are done here, my love."

Sally sighed. "Everywhere I turn, I seem to step on someone's toes," she said thoughtfully. "Your aunt and your cousin Annabella do not like me, and Gervais, I am sure, thinks me some sort of walking joke. When I went to inspect the kitchens, the servants gaped at me," she added thoughtfully. "I do feel something like a fish out of water, Peter."

Peter stroked her hair. "You'll learn. It takes time. And of course, it was very wretched of me not to tell them that I had married abroad and was bringing home a bride."

"Peter," Sally said slowly, "did you and Annabella ever—was there ever anything between you?"

Peter laughed. "Oh, it was only calf love," he said carelessly. "Before I went into the navy, you know, I fancied myself struck with her. But she, of course, wanted nothing to do with me. She was set upon making her come-out and having a title to add to her crown."

A small crease appeared between Sally's brows. If Peter had meant to be comforting, he had failed miserably. "And how do you feel, now that you've seen her again?" she asked.

Peter met her gaze with startled blue eyes. "How do I feel about her?" he repeated. Then he laughed. "Rather as if I cannot wait for us to be out of black gloves so that I can see her married off, and both her and Aunt Theresa safely established somewhere else beside Marchman Place." He nuzzled Sally's neck. "And then we can set about the business most pleasant of filling it with children of our own."

At that moment, Fishguard chose to fling open the library doors. "Lady Aurelia Fallon," he announced, apparently blind to the sight of Lord Marchman nibbling his own wife's neck at three o'clock in the afternoon.

Peter and Sally were still stumbling to their feet as a very tiny but no less imposing dowager in a sable pelisse swept into the room.

Sharp, small eyes like jet beads, set deep in the flesh on either side of a beaky nose, took the newlywed pair in, and the tiny mouth, perpetually pulled downward toward the several chins, opened slightly as this apparition marched majestically across the room. A tiny hand, gloved in black kid, was withdrawn from an enormous and ancient sable muff. "Well, Peter," Lady Aurelia said in frigid accents, "I see I find you well?"

Dutifully Peter bent and kissed the rouged and withered cheek. "Yes, Aunt Aurelia," he said with surprising meekness.

"And you," the dowager continued, looking up and down Sally's linen apron, "must be Lady Marchman."

"Yes, ma'am," Sally said, regarding Lady Aurelia cautiously. She wondered how anyone so small could give the impression of being quite so intimidating.

"You are, I apprehend, an American?" Lady Aurelia asked.

Sally nodded, unable to speak.

"I see," said the dowager. "Then that must explain why you are wearing an apron. It is not the fashion in England."

"I was wearing an apron because I was going through the books," Sally explained mildly.

"Bookish, are you? You'll be the first Marchman that ever was, if that's the case. Well, Peter, I offer you my felicitations."

"Thank you, Aunt Aurelia," he said.

"And I certainly wish you well of your task. Richard ran Marchman Place into the ground in a most deplorable fashion. I hope that you can contrive to bring it around. Tell me, Lady Marchman, did you bring a good dowry?"

"Respectable, ma'am," Sally said.

"Good, because the Marchmans need every penny they can get. I must tender my apologies for my late arrival, but my coach was beset by a highwayman, and it caused a great deal of trouble. Quite boring, I assure you."

"Highwaymen?" Peter asked, astonished.

The plumes in the dowager's bonnet nodded majestically. "A mere footpad, waving a rather vulgar pistol about in a most careless fashion! I gave him a piece of my mind, you may be certain."

In spite of himself, Peter's lips twitched. "Yes, ma'am, I may be certain that you did." To Sally he murmured, "Poor fellow!"

"One cannot but be aware that the times are difficult for many persons, but in one's day, highwaymen behaved with a great deal more style than they do today," the dowager said carelessly, drawing off her black gloves and her high-crowned hat. "I shall take it for granted that Fishguard has notified Theresa and Annabella of my arrival, and that tea shall be forthcoming."

"Not to mention your dear Gervais, ma'am," drawled that individual as he entered the library.

"Ah, yes. Gervais," Lady Aurelia said with no particular enthusiasm, although she did allow him to bend and place a kiss upon her cheek. "I see you are in fine fettle," she added with a glance at his waistcoat, a particularly elaborate example of its genre in celestial-blue silk, figured with butterflies.

"Well, Lady Marchman, don't stand there and gape at me as if I were one of the lions at Astley's, which I assure you I am not. You may escort me to the green salon, which, if my memory serves me well, is the single habitable room in this old pile," Lady Aurelia instructed. "And please do take off that apron before tea."

Sally did as she was told, offering Lady Aurelia her arm. "Just as you say, ma'am," she replied with composure. "And I shall give Fishguard orders to see that you and your maid are installed in the rose room. I believe its chimney does not smoke as badly as the others, and there you will be comfortable."

"Comfort!" Lady Aurelia snorted. "In my day, we thought of duty, not comfort." But she allowed Sally to take her arm, nonetheless, and lead her out of the room.

For once in total sympathy, Peter and Gervais exchanged a look.

"You know, I didn't expect Aunt Aurelia," Peter said a little sheepishly. "I knew Sally could deal with the rest of the family, but Aunt Aurelia—"

"Just so, old man," Gervais said easily. "No

one *expects* to deal with Aunt Aurelia! One lives in dread of it. Well, steady as she goes, Peter."

"Rather so."

Once she had entered the green salon, made some acerbic comment upon Theresa's still being in the habit of quacking herself, and remarked with asperity that Annabella had best come out of black gloves very soon, since gray was not becoming to her, by way of greeting her two female relations, Lady Aurelia allowed Sally to offer her the most comfortable chair by the fire and attend to her comfort. From this vantage point, her sharp little eyes seemed to miss nothing, and Sally was well aware that her manners were being assayed and evaluated as she lifted the heavy silver teapot to pour the amber liquid into a Lowestoft (sadly chipped) cup. Having ascertained that her husband's most ancient relation preferred milk and sugar, she added these and passed the cup to Gervais, who presented it to his aunt.

"Pretty pretty," she muttered, accepting the cup from Gervais' hands. "Whatever else they teach you in America, you know how to pour a dish of tea with credit."

Since Miss Henrietta would have perished from the face of the earth before allowing any daughter of hers to escape from Water Garden without this knowledge, Sally could only smile. "Well, I daresay we are not as savage as Peter would wish to make us sound, ma'am," she said smoothly, continuing to pour.

Aunt Aurelia snorted—or what sounded suspiciously like a snort to those assembled. "Very pretty," she remarked dryly.

A faint smile had appeared at the corners of Annabella's mouth. Terrified of her Aunt Aurelia, she could picture no event more fortuitous to furthering her plans than the unexpected arrival of that grande dame. The dowager was certain to disapprove of anyone who did not travel in the highest circles of the ton. Only see how she treated Gervais, and after Brummell, it was Gervais who set the fashion. A few blasts from Aunt Aurelia's withering tongue should be enough to scourge that know-it-all American miss. And certainly such a thing must make Peter think about her total ineligibility for the role to which he had elevated her. But Annabella had yet another plan up her sleeve. One, she hoped, that would serve to drive a wedge between Peter and Sally that nothing could loose.

Annabella never thought she would see the day come when she would be *glad* to see her Great-aunt Aurelia, but . . .

She smiled again and waited until there was a suitable lull in the teatime conversation.

"I have been thinking, you know, that since this is the last week that we should be in mourning, perhaps it would be a good idea to mark the event by introducing dear Sally to the neighborhood on Thursday next."

"Those that Uncle Richard did not make our blood-feud enemies!" Peter laughed. "He quarreled with everyone, you know. Even Prinny eventually left the house in high dudgeon."

"I would imagine that they'll come soon enough on Lady Marchman's invitation," Gervais drawled.

"Even the Prince Regent?" Sally asked, only half-seriously.

"Not him, not at this season," Gervais said.

"Anyway, Lady Marchman, you would hardly wish to have him. It is not at all the thing, you know," Lady Aurelia said. "An excellent idea,

Annabella. I trust that you will draw up the cards of invitation, Theresa, since you will be introducing Lady Marchman to your neighbors?"

"Me?" Aunt Theresa squeaked. "My health would never permit it."

"Oh, I shall do so, never fear. An evening party, I think, dinner and perhaps a little dancing after."

"So soon after mourning?" Aunt Aurelia asked in deep tones of disapproval.

"Oh, no waltzes, I assure you, ma'am! Just a few country dances, for the young people," Annabella said breathlessly. "After all, this is a happy time."

Aunt Aurelia gave a short nod of assent.

"I cannot tell you how fascinating it all sounds, dear cousin. Unfortunately, I have engagements in town which claim my attention," Gervais said lazily. "Else I should be delighted to stay and lead Lady Marchman out in the first reel."

"Nonsense, Gervais," Peter said. "You're just too town-bronzed to lend your fashionable self to a country party that I am sure you would consider a dead bore."

"As you wish, old man," Gervais replied lightly, touching his neckcloth with just the tip of one finger. "*I* shall not dispute you, now that you are the head of the family. But I do have engagements in town, nonetheless! Beginning of Season and all of that!"

"Oh, Gervais! And I was counting upon you!" Annabella sighed, batting her long lashes.

"Well, then, think again, dear cousin," Gervais said airily. "For it's off I must be."

This was better than Annabella had expected, and it was all she could do to keep from handing him his hat and coat right there. "What a pity," she sighed, "that you are too top-lofty for us here in the country."

"Wait until you come up to town, Annabella, and then tell me how top-lofty I am."

"I suppose you will be presenting Lady March-man at court?" Lady Aurelia demanded of Mrs. Marchman.

Aunt Theresa all but collapsed upon her couch at the thought. "My health . . . the strain . . . too much for sad invalid such as I . . ." And a great many other disjointed phrases besides. It was all her toes, ensconced in needlepoint slippers, could do not to turn up at the very thought.

"Well, she'll have to be presented now that she's a married lady," Aunt Aurelia said, turning her beady black eyes upon Sally.

"I had not thought about that," Peter said in such dubious tones that Sally had to steal a side-ways glance at him. "She's not prepared for that sort of boggle, you know."

For the first time, it occurred to Sally that she may have entered a world where she did not belong, and that perhaps Peter was having that same thought also. It was not a cheering thought, and unconsciously, she edged a little farther down the sofa, away from her husband.

"Of course, there's time enough to think about that when Marchman House is opened again. And you should, you know, because Annabella hasn't even had a full Season," Aunt Aurelia pronounced.

Peter shrugged. "Really, since I don't plan to live in fashionable society, I don't see how it would matter. And I don't think that Sally cares much one way or the other."

This statement only served to confirm Sally's

suspicions, and it was all she could do to keep herself from flushing quite red.

"Well, of course, we cannot expect Sally to have vouchers for Almack's," Annabella said. "But otherwise, we might expect to see her safely launched."

"And why couldn't she go to Almack's?" Peter demanded suddenly.

Annabella fluttered prettily. "Well, of course, I couldn't say, but you know how it is, Peter—"

"What Annabella's tryin' to say," Gervais put in, "is that Sally's an American, and our lofty patronesses are likely to look down their noses at her for that, correct, my dear cousin?"

Annabella had the grace to blush. "Well, not precisely, but now that you mention it, yes! I'm sorry, Sarah, but that is how it is," she added, overplaying her hand.

"I think I see, but what is this Almack's," Sally asked stiffly, "that I should feel so hurt if I were refused?"

"It is *the* place, of course, for fashionable society," Annabella exclaimed, much shocked. "I am sure that even in America, you must know about Almack's."

"It is a very dull place," Gervais said, "where one drags one's marriageable daughters to be seen by marriageable males. They only dance Scotch reels and country waltzes, nothing stronger than orangeat is served, and the doors close at eleven. A dead bore."

"But very important, if one is to be socially acceptable, you see," Annabella said earnestly.

"I see," Sally repeated.

"Well, I don't. Bloody dreary sort of place," Peter said.

"Almack's may be a bloody, dreary sort of place,

Peter, but you must admit that vouchers are far more important than a court presentation!" Annabella sent her little shaft home, all innocence.

"Well, I don't care to go to London anyway," Peter said at last. "So I would imagine that that pretty well settles that."

Sally stared down into her teacup, frowning. She suddenly felt deeply uncomfortable.

10

After a stiff afternoon, followed by what Sally could only think of as an interminable dinner and an evening rendered only slightly less hideously dull by Gervais' dry and witty conversation, Lord and Lady Marchman, following the dowager's lead, retired to bed early.

Peter's conversation was still riddled with farm problems, even in pillow talk. In the ordinary course of events, Sally would have lent an ear, and perhaps even have tendered some very good advice. But after the events of teatime and the descent upon Marchman Place of Lady Aurelia, her mind had been driven elsewhere, and it was with a thin dry edge that she asked Peter: "Does your family see me as being unacceptable in their circles?"

Peter, who had been discoursing upon the number of bushels of wheat that could reasonably be expected to yield per acre, stopped in midsentence. "What?" he asked.

Sally rolled over and propped herself up on her elbow. "I asked you, do you think your family considers me socially unacceptable?"

"Whatever makes you think that? Of course, you haven't been born and bred to all of this the way Annabella has, but I'm sure that she's doing her best to give you an idea of how you should go on," Peter said innocently.

"Annabella tell me how I should go on?" Sally demanded. "Annabella has no more idea of household management than a titmouse!"

Peter placed a hand against Sally's shoulder. "There, now, Sally, don't go on in such a way. Annabella means well, I am sure. If she seems officious, it is only because she is trying to show you how things are done."

"And how would you have liked it if one of my brothers were to make such comments about your inability to attend the Santimoke Assemblies because you were English? *I* should say such a thing was very rude."

Peter laughed. "Is that what you are up in the boughs about, my love? I should not give it a second thought. What do you care for fashionable parties and London life? We have Marchman Place to straighten out first, you know." He yawned, which was not precisely the reaction that Sally wanted.

"No, you are quite right, Peter, I don't care for what is fashionable in London, and I hope that it will never be said of a Goldsborough of Water Garden that she cared what was said about her by some milk-and-water miss. I simply want to know if you share your cousin's feelings that I won't do."

But Peter was sound asleep, exhausted from a long day's work. With a muffled exclamation of disgust, Sally turned over on her side and pulled the counterpane up around her head.

In the days that followed, Sally saw very little of her husband. He was up at daybreak and out upon his land, putting himself to the task of attempting to restore his inheritance to its former glory. When he did come in, the only moments they had alone were those in the marital bedchamber, and by the time Peter had laid down, he was quickly off to sleep.

Sally's days were filled with Peter's relations, whose subtle barbs she was deeply conscious of feeling, in spite of Annabella's professed volteface. She was genuinely distressed when Gervais took his leave of them on Tuesday, feeling as if she had lost her only ally.

Perhaps Gervais felt the same emotion, for as he was throwing himself up into his high-perch phaeton beside his valet, he leaned down and whispered into Sally's ear, "If you ever decide that you need to contrive to be brought into London fashion, Sally, send for me!"

At the time, she smiled weakly, thinking it a jest, but she could not know that very soon there would come a time when she would recall his words.

Since Sally was almost wholly preoccupied with what she was beginning to feel to be a losing battle to present Marchman Place as something at least resembling a well-managed household, she was content to leave the directions for the party completely in Annabella's hands. "I would not even know whom to invite," Sally said frankly.

"Leave it all to me," Annabella purred, and set to sending cards of invitation to selected persons in the neighborhood.

Lady Aurelia could never be said to judge or comment, yet Sally felt her intimidating presence quite as much as, if not more than, that of Mrs. Marchman and Annabella. It was not that she became sycophantic toward the formidable dowager; in fact, quite the contrary; she said and did precisely what she would in any circumstance. Unlike Annabella, Sally did not have a number of personalities at her disposal that she could switch at will.

Indeed, if Sally was intimidated by the subtle snobbery of the Marchmans, she gave no one the least outward hint. Her only attempt to discuss the matter had been with Peter, and that had been futile.

Instead, she went about what she thought to be her true business, and by the end of the week, between herself and Mrs. Gunning, Marchman Place was no longer dusty and encrusted with age. Everything gleamed with wax and polish, and characteristics of fine old pieces, long tarnished and dull, were suddenly recalled as if they had been new again.

"It quite gives the place a new tone," Fishguard was heard to say to Mrs. Gunning belowstairs with approval.

By Thursday afternoon, the entire house was thrown into an upheaval by the prospect of entertaining guests, even so small a number as twenty couples. As has been noted, the late Uncle Richard had managed to quarrel with half the neighborhood, and even in his most convivial days as a crony of Prinny, had never brought anyone to Marchman Place out of the hunting season.

This, therefore, was an important event in the lives of those above and belowstairs, as well as the entire neighborhood, for not an invitation was extended that was not accepted, and listening to Annabella bandying about the titles, Sally was inclined to think that the woods must be quite thick with peerages in the West Country.

There was a great deal of activity in the kitchen,

and the musicians arrived at teatime from Ottery
Saint Mary, setting up in the ballroom and rendering Mrs. Marchman's repose in the room directly above hideous.

A red carpet was unearthed from some deep
recess of an attic, and the two footmen, under
Fishguard's supervision, rolled it out from the
portals of the hall, down the worn stone steps,
and out into the drive.

The dining room, having undergone a thorough
cleaning from top to bottom, so that the cruets
shone as bright as the chandeliers, was laid out
with every piece of silver in the Marchman collection, awaiting the seating of elegant diners.

Sally was in conference with Mrs. Gunning
when Annabella bustled importantly into the
room. "*There* you are!" she exclaimed. "You must
come at once and get ready, you know, or you
won't be down to greet the first guests, would
never do."

Her smile was so expansive that Sally relaxed
her guard. "I suppose you are right. After all,
Annabella, this is your party."

Annabella's smile exhibited a great many white
teeth. "Oh, no, my dear, this is your party. The
whole neighborhood is simply pining to meet you,
after all."

She hustled Sally upstairs and into the bedroom, where a housemaid was just finishing pouring the last can of hot water into the shoe bath.
"That will be all, Rose. I shall wait on Lady
Marchman myself," Annabella said firmly.

Rose, who had been serving as Lady Marchman's
maid pro temp, gave Annabella a suspicious look.
"Out!" Annabella hissed, and the maid scurried
through the door.

"Now, my dear cousin, if you will just bathe

yourself, I will look through your wardrobe and choose a suitable dress. Tonight, you know, you must wear the Marchman jewels."

"The Marchman jewels?" Sally asked, raising her eyebrows a little.

"Of course. Every Lady Marchman wears them. It is traditional to wear them the very first time you entertain as Lady Marchman, you know," Annabella said from the dressing room, where she could be heard going through the clothes-press, looking at Sally's clothes.

"What sort of jewels?" Sally asked, slipping out of her muslin dress and untying her garters.

"Ah! I'm afraid they're nothing like what they have in the really grand old families, you know, great big stones going back to the Conquest, but they are quite respectable, I assure you! There's a diamond and emerald diadem, and a necklace with emeralds and diamonds and pearls, and some earrings, emeralds and diamonds, and a pair of bracelets. They're very Georgian and old-fashioned, you know. Our great-grandmother had them reset—well, you'll see!" Annabella promised breathlessly. "Are you in your bath yet?"

"Almost," Sally replied, undoing her stay laces. "I had no idea this was supposed to be such a formal gathering tonight. In the country and all of that."

"Oh, yes. I assure you that upon times like this, we are depressingly, gothicly formal. It is what is expected of us, after all! I say, this red velvet is just the thing."

"Red velvet? In June?" Sally asked, dipping a cautious toe into the water. "I should rather think not."

"Oh, yes! Absolutely! And it will look so bang

up to the knocker with the emeralds, too," Annabella cooed. "Do trust me, Sarah."

Precisely at eight, Sally picked up her train, touched one of the heavy earrings to be certain it was in place, took a deep breath, and began to descend the staircase.

Fishguard, standing at attention in the hallway, looked up at her. For a moment, his careful professional demeanor seemed to be seriously distorted to the point where his jaw dropped into his cravat. Twenty years in service stood him in good stead, however, for the next moment, his countenance was schooled in a rigidly correct expression, and his voice was completely devoid of any emotion as he said, "Good evening, my lady. My lord is entertaining Sir Julian and Lady Chombley in the green salon."

"Thank you," Sally said nervously, kicking her velvet train as she dragged it like a ball and chain down the endless hollow stone corridor toward that chamber. Whatever Annabella might say, she could not help but feel that velvet, and in June, was a bit much for a simple country party.

At the heavy oak doors of the green salon, she paused almost wishing she could retreat back up the stairs again to her own room. For a single moment, she considered pleading a sick headache, but Sally Goldsborough had been brought up to know her duty, and so, with an inward sigh, she turned the heavy iron knob and made her entrance.

"Ah!" Peter said, turning from a mild-looking rural couple, "May I present ... my wife ..." His voice trailed away, and the happy smile on his face was replaced by a look of consternation.

His expression was all that Sally needed to

know that she had done something terribly gauche. If he had exclaimed, "See my American wife who does not know how to go on," it could not have been borne in upon her more strongly that she was miserably *de trop*.

She felt as if she must look like a vulgar trollop to the many pairs of eyes that surveyed her carefully from head to foot. The velvet gown, heavily laiden with gold embroidery and cut extremely décolleté, in an unflattering shade of rose red, was better suited to a function in the White House or the Palace than a simple country dinner among friends and relations, and not another woman in the room wore any jewel more elaborate than a string of good pearls or a pair of diamond earbobs. The full and ornate weight of the Marchman jewels stuck to her perspiring flesh, glittering too loudly and too ornately by contrast. Her strawberry hair, which was usually dressed in two simple bands, had been, at Annabella's command, taken to with the curling irons to produce a pair of overlarge sidecurls and a great many swirls and dips and cupid's knots upon which to rest the large diadem, which was digging into her scalp. Annabella's final touch, to dip into the powder and rouge pots with a generous hand, insisting that Sally's freckles must be cleared away, must make her look like a painted corpse by contrast to these fresh English complexions.

If she could have sunk into the floor at that moment, Sally would have gladly done so. How vulgar and common they must all think her now, Sally realized terribly, her smile glued horribly to her face.

At that moment, the door opened again, and Annabella, in a simple silk dinner gown swept into the room. For just a moment, her eyes met Sally's, and a flicker of malicious triumph passed through her eyes as she gracefully moved to greet the guests.

Sally stood rooted to the spot, two bright spots of color appearing in her cheeks as she understood Annabella's clever game. Awkwardly, when Peter prodded her, she moved forward to greet Sir Julian and Lady Chombley, humiliated by the politely concealed curiosity in their eyes.

Peter's American wife! How all their suspicions and prejudices must be confirmed! Lord, they would go home and laugh at her for a country hick, no more fit to be Lady Marchman than a wild Indian. Desperately, she cast about her for some way to excuse herself, to run upstairs and change her dress. But even as she was about to speak, Fishguard was opening the door again, to announce yet more guests, rendering change impossible.

Feeling quite sunk below reproach as lady after lady appeared in the simplest of evening dresses, many of them even a season or two out of style, Sally raised her chin and put up the best front she could, concealing her agony of embarrassment and avoiding Peter's eye. Doubtless, her manners must seem stiff and formal, she thought, as if she were, on top of all else, putting on airs she thought suited her station as a baroness, but it could not be helped, and her smile felt like papier-mâché, it was so stiff and unnatural as she shook hand after hand, trying not to see their startled looks. Lady Somebody, Lord Somewhatelse, Mr. and Mrs. Whomever, Sir Someone. It seemed as if they would never stop coming with their slightly lifted brows and their speaking looks at the Marchman emeralds.

All too aware of Peter's disapproval and Annabella's smug expression of triumph, Sally could
only wish that Gervais were here to save the day.

Direct and frank as Sally was, such a piece of
treachery as Annabella had played upon her
seemed almost inconceivably cruel, but she had
only to look at the beauty to know that it was a
well-thought-out plan, and to know, sickeningly,
the reason why. She only had to see the way
Annabella murmured in Peter's ear, or laid a
hand upon his arm to understand what had inspired this piece of work.

Her heart sank into her slippers when Lady
Aurelia made her entrance into the room. Watching those sharp, hawklike eyes taking in every
detail of her toilette, from the tip of her damask
striped toes to the cupid's knots in her hair,
Sally knew that that thin little mouth was purs-
ing in preparation for a sharp setdown.

Wordlessly, the tiny dowager, in puce silk and
a black turban, moved like a queen across the
room and looked up into Sally's eyes.

Sally trembled a little, but evidently, whatever
Lady Aurelia read in Sally's expression told her
all she needed to know, for she laughed a deep,
rolling Georgian laugh and playfully slapped Sally's arm with her fan sticks.

"Here, now, my dear," she said loudly, "I do
think that we have had our little joke." Was it
Sally's imagination, or did one lid drop over a
beady black eye for a split second. Certainly,
everyone in the room had now given Lady Aurelia their full attention, and perhaps that was
what she wanted.

Reaching up on tiptoe, she removed the diadem and the heavy earbobs from Sally. "I shall
now well and truly owe you that cashmere shawl

of mine, my dear Sarah, and I hope it may teach me from now on, that when I bet with you, it shall only be at silver loo for chicken stakes!" The old lady loosened enough to chuckle indulgently as she undid the heavy necklace from about Sally's neck. Looking about the room, Lady Aurelia permitted the guests one of her small, so very condescending smiles. "Dear Sarah grew quite incensed with me for saying that I doubted that Americans had the dash to play jokes, and so I staked her my Madras cashmere shawl that she would not make her entrance tonight in costume. She chose the Empress Josephine, and I must say, she's done a nacky sort of a job of it. Why, only a fortnight ago, Sally Jersey appeared at one of Princess Lieven's parties dressed as a milkmaid, and now the poor princess must stand her a gown from Celeste's!" The dowager patted Sally's arm affectionately. "Wonderful gel, perfectly wonderful. Peter's chosen very nicely in his American bride."

Since the old lady was known everywhere to be a very high stickler indeed, as well as a female who moved in the most fashionable London circles, this explanation, however rackety, was easily accepted by all those present, and relieved laughter could be detected here and there. Aside from which, who would dare to argue with so formidable a personage as Lady Aurelia?

"Now, dear, having proven your point, do run upstairs and slip into your dinner gown," Lady Aurelia commanded. "And, yes, Peter, I should like a glass of sherry thank you very much. Charlotte, my dear, increasing again?"

Annabella's look was so much like that of a thwarted baby that as Sally passed from the room, she could not help but smile.

The rest of the evening passed off without too many untoward incidents, and Sally, suitably regroomed and attired in a simple silk jonquil gown with net overskirt and rosebud sleeves, passed herself off quite credibly as a protégée of Miss Henrietta's tutelage. A dinner, a simple five courses with twenty removes, was cooked well and served without mishap, and the glass of wine Fishguard poured for her relaxed her just enough to prove herself both witty and charming to her dinner partners. Years of interaction with the colonel and his cronies had taught her exactly what landowning gentlemen liked to talk about, which was to say she only had to probe their interests with a few questions and, once guided, sit back and listen attentively as they discoursed upon their favorite subjects over ham and chutney pickle.

When the sorbet had been removed and the last of the fruit in the silver epergne had been picked over by persons who swore they couldn't eat another bite, Sally gracefully rose from the table. "I think it is the custom everywhere," she announced, "to leave you gentlemen to your port and cigars and scandalous stories while we ladies repair to our marsala, biscuits, and scandalous stories. But I must warn you not to keep us waiting too long, or we shall all be in costume when you join us."

Thus able to laugh at herself, Sally looked down the table at Peter. His face was dark and flushed, and he was leaning back in his chair, his fingers wrapped about his wineglass. The look he shot her was not, she noted unhappily, a happy one, or even a friendly one.

But there were appreciative chuckles from other members of the dinner party, and as she lead the way out of the gloomy dining room, she overheard Lady Chombley whispering to Mrs. Marchman. "Delightful girl, Theresa. Good company for you and Annabella."

"She is," Mrs. Marchman sighed in die-away accents, "quite American. Rather exhausting." With a long-suffering sigh, Mrs. Marchman allowed a footman to assist her in rising from the table, trailing the demitrain of her gray and white silk over the dusty floor. "I eat like a bird," she moaned, and the footman, who had seen her put away just as much as the squire, suppressed a smile.

Lady Chombley raised an eyebrow. A pronounced countrywoman with a great penchant for the sporting life, she had little patience with Mrs. Marchman's ill health. "What you need, Theresa, is to get out-of-doors more often. Garden! Ride! Take walks! Visit the tenants! Take an interest! Buck you right up!"

Mrs. Marchman looked as if she would faint at the very idea. "I wonder if I left my Beccham's Cordial upstairs?" she wondered, digging about in her reticule.

As Sally led her little procession toward the green salon, she fell into step beside Lady Aurelia, moving at a stately pace down the cool stone hallway.

"Ma'am, I owe you everything! I—I was ill-advised—and mortified! I thought that you would never—that is—"

Lady Aurelia cut her small dark eyes upward at Sally. It may have been the younger woman's imagination but a faint upward curve appeared on her lips. "You thought that I would never take to an American miss bein' the new Lady Marchman? I'm not sayin' that I didn't come up here expectin' the worst, mind you, but I'm the sort who either takes a fancy to someone or don't. Daresay it's an odious habit, but I'm too old, too tired, and too rich to stop now. Thought you were pluck to the backbone when I first clapped eyes on you. Daresay your mama's a lady, and you've been brought up to be a lady too."

Thinking of Miss Henrietta, Sally's eyes misted slightly. "Yes, ma'am, my mother is a lady. A *real* lady."

Lady Aurelia nodded in satisfaction. "Breeding tells. Late husband said it about his horses; I say it about people. No need to tell me who got you up like a Covent Garden nun, because I can guess on." Lady Aurelia gave an eloquent sniff. "Never did take a fancy to that one. Spoiled—what's more, devious. Don't care for devious people, never did. Now, you take my butler, Duddle. Came to me when Lord Robert and I first set up housekeeping. Always tells me exactly what he's thinking, and don't mince words, either. Well, I've had them that's said, why do you keep him on, he's insolent. Well, I keep him on because he's honest, and many's the mistake he's kept me from making by speaking right up." She nodded firmly. "I've a mind to give that great-niece of mine a sharp set-down, you know."

"Oh, pray do not," Sally begged earnestly. "It will only make it all that much worse."

"Never fancied herself in love with Peter until he came into the title. Spoiled beauties. Seen it often enough. That Milbanke chit and Byron—"

Aunt Aurelia's jaw worked and she mulled over that recent and unfortunate scandal. Since Sally was ignorant of the personal life of the poet, she had nothing to contribute, and the old lady continued, "Thing of it is, when I saw you all tuckered up in those silly jewels and that gown, I knew that little ninny had something to do with it. That's when I decided that I would take one of my fancies to you, my girl." She nodded rather fiercely. "Not only do I like you, but I enjoy putting Theresa's nose out of joint. Have a fancy to leave everything to you, rather than Annabella. I *like* you!"

In spite of herself, Sally's lips twitched. "Thank you, ma'am, and I like you too, even if you *do* frighten me a little!"

"I like to frighten people. Keeps 'em in line. I wasn't rich, I wasn't pretty, and I wasn't particularly clever, you know. But I married Lord Robert and became a frightening old dragon in a turban, and the terror of my nieces and nephews and a great many other people. Don't tell anyone, my gel, but underneath, I'm charlotte russe."

"I won't, but I hope that you will live a great many more years and be just as grand as you are now," Sally confided. "For I would much rather have you than your inheritance!"

"Don't be too certain of that. It's a very grand inheritance. I'm full of brass," Lady Aurelia replied. "Now, get me a seat by the fire and a glass of that marsala, my gel! Exhaustin' thing, country parties!"

Meekly, Sally did as she was told, oblivious to the shocked looks exchanged between Annabella and her mother at this evidence that Lady Aurelia had taken one of her odd fancies to the American chit.

While Sally poured out tea and offered sweet biscuits about to her guests, Mrs. Marchman made a grand production of stretching herself out upon her chaise, covering herself with a number of shawls, and spooning the contents of various bottles between her lips, declining offers of assistance with a sad, sweet smile that proclaimed her the martyred invalid who could only be persuaded to drink two cups of heavily creamed and sugared tea and six or eight macaroons. "Well, if no one wants the last one on the plate," she sighed, popping it into her mouth.

Lady Chombley and Mrs. Rand-Perrot, having discovered that Sally was a horsewoman, immediately invited her to hunt their pack. "Of course, it's humbug country," Lady Chombley boomed, "but Chombley keeps a string at Melton, and if you and Peter should like to be our guests there this fall, I think you'll see good sport."

"If only I could have brought my own horse over," Sally was saying thoughtfully. "I am ashamed to say that after my family, I miss Thunder the most of all. But I suppose when Peter has pulled the estates into order, perhaps then we may think of horses." Her voice was a trace wistful.

"Well, there you are, my dear, you're welcome to come to Greycourt and pick any horse out that you might like," Lady Chombley exclaimed, laying a hand on Sally's knee. "We'll ride."

Very soon, Sally had been offered vouchers to the Assemblies, a place on the Altar Guild, and some clippings of a very fine rosebush from the legendary gardens at Younger Place, all of which served to convince her that her new neighbors were not so very different from the people she had left at home—good, honest people with a great love of the land and the simple pleasures of the country. With these people, she could be happy and content, she thought, warm in the glow of their acceptance.

Shortly after they had all entered the green

salon, a sullen, petulant expression had begun to settle down about Annabella's face. Some of it may have had to do with the fact that she was one of those women who cannot long endure without the company and admiration of men, but to a shrewd observer, like Lady Aurelia, it seemed in large part inspired by the fact that the new Lady Marchman's neighbors had warmed to her in a way that they had never warmed to Annabella, even the girls of her own age. Or, perhaps, particularly the girls of her own age.

Elaborately, she seated herself at the piano and began to play some dreary ballad, fretting at the keys and sighing impatiently every few minutes.

When Lady Aurelia sharply asked her to play more softly, lest no one be able to hear themselves, much less one another, she flounced off to sit in the window seat, sulking and ignored.

Sally felt a wave of pity for the beauty in spite of herself. What Annabella needed, she thought, was another Season in London. For her, the lights and the gaiety, the courting and flirting were life and breath itself. It seemed cruel and unnatural to keep her cooped up here in the country, mooning after Peter.

But Annabella came very close to destroying what small sympathy she had gained with Sally when the gentlemen, redolent of cigars and rosy with port, finally joined the ladies. Almost immediately, Annabella came to life, blooming under male attention.

Sally could have watched even this, amused, had not some benighted young man with spots begged Annabella to play the pianoforte for them.

"Of course I shall," she exclaimed, laughing and rosy, as she reached out and grasped Peter's arm, dragging him away from a deep conversation about ditching he was having with two other gentlemen, "if only Peter shall turn the pages for me, just as he used to do in the old days."

If Sally was hoping that Peter would look annoyed, or make some excuse, she was wrong, for he smiled, pushing his hands through his curls. "I see that I am commanded, gentlemen," he exclaimed, striding across the room to take his place by the instrument.

Mrs. Marchman sniffed approvingly into her handkerchief. "We had hoped, you know ..." she murmured to the vicar's wife.

Peter's face was flushed. Clearly, he had added port to the list of what he had had to drink that night, Sally thought uneasily, for as he bent over the pianoforte to adjust Annabella's music, their faces almost met, and she looked up at him in such a way that Mrs. Marchman stirred uneasily, aware that even her lax standards of propriety had been transgressed. Someone coughed, and Sally found the fan in her lap very interesting.

Annabella played a little trill, and began to sing, in a thin, rather melodramatic voice, a sad little ballad about a lass whose man has married another. If it had not been ludicrous, Sally thought, it would have been heartbreaking. But even the most devoted of Annabella's beaux looked distinctly uncomfortable, and the tip of the dowager's cane was tapping ominously against the floor.

Only Peter, in his cups, as were most of the gentlemen, seemed oblivious to Annabella's dubious choices in balladry. He leaned negligently against the piano, his back to the company, turning the pages at her doe-eyed nod, tapping his toe to the rhythm. Sally was amused to find herself more annoyed at Annabella's rather clumsy fingering than anything else. An excellent musician herself, she was barely tolerant of those less gifted, and wondered that Mrs. Marchman had not hired a harp master instead, since Annabella would have appeared to far better advantage in a Grecian bend over a large, gilted harp.

"Well," said Lady Aurelia firmly after the third or fourth ballad about blighted love, "music's all very well for them that likes, but I prefer my box at the opera or my subscription to the society. Did Fishguard say there were card tables set up in the library? Vicar? Sir Julian, a rubber or two?"

Standing before Sally, she murmured, from the corner of her mouth, "If you don't know how to play cards, gel, you're going to learn before you're many minutes older."

Apparently, a great many of the guests shared the dowager's sentiments, particularly the older members of the party, for there was a general exodus in the direction of the library.

Sally, faithfully following her mentor's advice, adjourned to the cards and dice box, without so much as a backward look toward her husband and his cousin, smiling as if it were all a grand joke, when she yearned to box the girl's ears and show her how the pianoforte ought to be played. What she wished to show Peter was more obscure, but she was a Goldsborough, and she had her pride.

11

An hour after the last coach had rolled down the drive and the last tallow candle extinguished in the servants' quarters, Lady Marchman sat before her dressing table, dragging a silver brush through her strawberry hair. Beneath her Chinese dressing gown, her spine was as straight and erect as either Miss Henrietta or Lady Aurelia could have wished a lady's posture to be. But that and the fire that shot from her eyes were dangerous signs.

The hated velvet dress was wadded into a ball and thrown into a corner of her dressing room behind the armoire. The rest of her garments lay strewn about as if she had disrobed while she were pacing the room and had let them lie where they fell, an untidiness that neither Miss Henrietta nor Lady Aurelia would have approved.

The two bright spots of color in her cheeks had nothing to do with the rouge pot that lay overturned across her dressing table, nor did the sheet-white pallor of the rest of her flesh come from the lead powder in the box spilling across the rug.

Beneath her breath, Sally hummed tunelessly, the main reason being that her teeth were clamped firmly together behind her tight lips.

Hearing a noise on the landing, she paused in

her brushing, listening as a hunter listens in the woods: Annabella's little giggle and Peter's deep careless laugh.

Her grip tightened on the handle of the brush for a moment, and then with a supreme effort, she continued her strokes.

In the bedroom, she heard the door open and close, and Peter's sigh as he removed his shoes. He really should have a valet, she thought absurdly, realizing what a "married" thought it was.

"So." He appeared in the doorway, leaning carelessly against the frame. In the mirror she could see that his cravat was undone and hanging loosely about his neck, and the buttons of his waistcoat open. There was a ladder in one of his black silk stockings, and a splash of red wine on his shirtfront. His dark curls were disheveled, his pale-blue eyes surrounded by bloodshot white.

"So," Sally said coldly, not looking around. He was rather drunk, which always made him argumentative. She supposed he and his guests had put away three or four bottles apiece; such was the way men drank, and were expected to drink, when they got together.

"I hope you will tell me what sort of a cake you made of yourself in that dress and the family jewels, ma'am," he said stiffly, haughty, playing the young lord.

"Marriage *à la mode*," Sally said to herself, thinking of a series of Hogarth prints she had once seen depicting the decline of a marriage just as this one. Her hand tightened on the hairbrush. "I was ill-advised as to what was appropriate attire," she said in her matter-of-fact voice, since she had discovered that drove him mad.

"I would say that you were. You looked like

one of Mother Goody's tarts. Good God, Sal, did you have to embarrass me in front of the entire neighborhood?"

"Why? So they would all think me—an American? Someone who eats with her fingers, perhaps, or wears skins and feathers? Someone who married you for your title and your money, perhaps?" Now she did turn to look at him, and thought she saw the barb hit home. "That has been what you've been thinking, hasn't it, Peter?" She was surprised at the calm sound of her own voice. "You've come home to merrie old England, and now, in your own world your provincial American bride doesn't seem quite as sweet to you as she did when she paroled you out of jail in Maryland, does she?"

He winced, putting up his hands, as if he could deflect her words. "It's not like that," he muttered, looking down at his stocking feet uncertainly. "I still love you, Sally—"

"But I simply don't fit in, do I?" Sally asked coolly, picking up an orange stick with shaking hands and pushing it beneath her nails. "Now that you're Lord Marchman, you wish that you had married a proper Englishwoman to make you a proper baroness. One who knows how to go on at Marchman Place. Someone like your cousin, perhaps."

"I knew you'd drag that in," Peter said sullenly, hanging his head in a guilty way. "Sally, she don't signify to me, not the way you do."

"My, you certainly could have fooled me and about sixteen other people this evening," Sally replied airily, tearing at her cuticles. "I must say the way you were leaning over her dismal little set of songs at the pianoforte must have made the entire neighborhood wonder why you married me. It certainly can't be my ten thousand dollars in gold, since you consider dollars so paltry against the pound sterling."

"She's my cousin," Peter grumbled sullenly, pushing his hands into his pockets and curling up his toes. "Known her ever since she was in leading strings. Like a sister!"

Sally cocked an eyebrow. "A most unnatural sister, then, sir." She was trying to keep her voice down.

"A schoolgirl crush!"

"Annabella is well past the age of the schoolroom, as well you know, Peter. Understanding that a beautiful, lively, and rather, well, devious female should not be kept on a short chain out here in the country, when she should be in London having another Season, flirting and courting with every eligible buck in town and having a grand time, with pretty new clothes and lots of dancing and parties, does not excuse the little piece of nastiness she practiced on me tonight! More fool I for listening to her."

"She's high-spirited," Peter excused, looking sheepish.

"High-spirited, my stars and garters, if you will pardon my decidedly unfashionable Americanism. Why is it that men will excuse anything, up to and including homicide, of a pretty woman? What Annabella is, husband mine, is a spoiled, selfish, vain deceitful little brat who needs to be married off to a man who will endure her personality for the sake of her looks."

"Well, it was a damned good joke," Peter muttered defensively. "Wish you could have seen your face."

"I wish you could have seen yours. To you, it

was definitely not a jest, when you thought that I knew no better than to appear in company in such a quiz," Sally exclaimed, stung. "Good God, Peter, have some sense, no matter how foxed you are! It would never do in country society for the new Lady Marchman to be considered vulgar and unmannered. We must live with these people, and with the estates in such bad shape, it behooves us to do everything in our power to be certain to remain on good terms with our neighbors, not setting me up as a Halloween fright! That can only make us both appear eccentric and unstable. Hardly a portrait *I* should wish to paint of Lord and Lady Marchman at any time. And particularly when, upon the whole, your neighbors appear to me to be decent, honest people who are anxious to see you succeed. Lord knows, they must have imagined almost anything when they heard I was an American." Sally smiled bitterly. "I do not need Annabella's jealousy to confirm their worst suspicions of me! Good God, one might think an American were a Hottentot, or a Martian the way your family acts toward me." Sensing she had gone too far, Sally pressed a hand against her lips, shaking her head. Bad enough to have to say anything about Annabella, let alone the rest of his relations.

If Peter had been listening to her speech, he gave no indication, merely lifted his wineglass to his lips and emptied the dregs. "Annabella," he sighed, inclining his head against the doorframe and looking at his wife's angry face, "why, I do believe you're jealous," he slurred, smiling loosely, in just that way that would irritate Sally the most.

"If I am, it is because you have given me reason to be so." She rose from the vanity, drawing her robe around her as she paced the room, her freckles standing out against the pallor of her skin. She knew she should restrain her tongue, but weeks of enduring every slight and sly innuendo had roused her temper. Slow to anger, when she was finally pushed to explode, she was formidable. "Since the minute I walked into this house, your hypochondriac aunt and your—your *bitch*, forgive me, but there is no other word—of a cousin have done everything in their power to belittle me, to make me feel unwelcome and—and totally unsuitable to be your wife, to be Lady Marchman. Clearly, it is their belief that I am unskilled in managing servants, holding household, entertaining, or in any way possessing the attributes suitable to a baroness. Whatever they might be! If it means lying about on the sofa all day quacking yourself, or flirting with everything in pants, then perhaps I am. We were not brought up that way at Water Garden, after all. But Water Garden is so provincial and frontier—of course, I forget! My accent, my manners, my clothes, my conversation, and I daresay even my seat—if I had a horse to sit—would not be up to their standards. Clearly, Annabella fills these admirably, since it has been made clear to me a hundred times that she was raised to fill the role."

Having vented her rage, Sally sank down on the chaise, pressing her hands to her cheeks. "Oh! I am sorry. I did not mean to say anything at all," she whispered, much ashamed of her outburst. "Gervais and Aunt Aurelia have been everything that is good and kind to me."

"Yes, I note that you have managed to ingratiate yourself with that fop cousin of mine, and that my Great-aunt Aurelia has taken one of her capricious fancies to you! You are to be congratulated upon two such notable conquests," Peter remarked dryly. "I am, however, very sorry that you have taken such a dislike to my Aunt Theresa and my cousin Annabella. Aunt Theresa is a harmless, sick old woman with no other place to go. Annabella—Annabella is my oldest friend and playmate. You judge her harshly in your jealousy. She may be high-spirited, but—"

"*High-spirited?*" Sally exclaimed, in tones of horror. "I suppose, then, sir, that Lady Macbeth was vaporish?"

She knew that she was being quite vindictive; she also knew it was a losing battle to attempt to reason with Peter when he had been drinking too much. At Water Garden, when people argued, they shouted and slammed doors, working toward the moment when common sense and compromise would restore order. It was her only experience of disagreement, and she expected that this, her first argument with Peter, would end the same way, for she knew no other.

A bit rubberishly, he drew himself up to his full height, looking down at her with cold ice-blue eyes, his lips set in a hard tight line. If he had not looked so silly, she might have instinctively noticed the warning signals and tried a more peacemaking tack. As it was, she glanced coldly back, crossing her arms stubbornly across her chest.

"Madam," Peter said in awful tones, as if he were a rather bad actor in a rather indifferent play, "when you married me, you married into my family. If you do not like them, that is your privilege and right. Actually," he added in a drunkenly confidential tone, "I don't like any of my relatives very much myself, and you haven't met the third and fourth cousins—pack of loose screws." Recovering himself, he continued in his bad-actor voice, "My Aunt Theresa is the relict of one of my uncles. She has had no other home since her marriage but Marchman Place. Annabella, my cousin Annabella has grown up here. Born here. Lived here all her life. As the head of the family, I would like to see her marry from here. This is their home, madam. And has been for far longer than it has been yours. If you cannot learn to live in some sort of relative harmony with them, perhaps you ought to remove yourself to the Dower House."

Sally glared at him. "Maybe I shall," she announced. "Then you and Annabella may do whatever you like, with Aunt Theresa looking on with the vapors."

"Maybe you're right," he said, trying for cold dignity and achieving only the clownishness of the truly intoxicated. "Maybe I should have married Annabella. She wouldn't always be after a fellow when he's breaking his back trying to pull these damned estates up from the River Tick with no more knowledge of how to go on than a babe unborn, expecting him to sit and chat when he's dead tired from mending a barn roof or plowing a field, or digging a half-mile of postholes, or nursing a cow through a difficult calfing or—or any of the hundred and eighty things I awaken every morning to find on my plate. Maybe she wouldn't come bearing tales of squabbling relations and hidden pranks to a man's had a few with his friends and only wants his bed because he's got to be up at five tomorrow to plan where some drainage ditches must be dug so the barley fields won't flood." Wearily, he leaned against the doorway, in love with the tired sound of his own voice. "Maybe she'd appreciate the fact that I'm trying to repair the damage done by three generations of squeezing every last groat from the land without putting a penny back into it. Maybe she'd appreciate the fact that I didn't set out to be Lord Marchman, that what I thought about was a wife in a sunbonnet, and me in buckskins, heading out to Ohio territory in a wagon to carve out our own place from that vast American wilderness, instead of crimping and shifting and slaving over land that's been leeched out for five hundred years."

At another time, in another mood, Sally might have been moved by such a speech. As it was, she could only control her anger enough to say, somewhat bitterly, "If only I were not trapped in this house all day with such a pair! Every time I wish to see something set to rights, even something as simple as repairing the sash in the blue salon, or pulling up that overgrown rose garden and starting fresh and clean, they roll their eyes and sigh at me until I feel that having the curtains in the dining room washed disturbs centuries of tradition. I would be of more help outside in the fields." She turned her wedding band about on her hand. "When all is said and done, I *am* a farmer's daughter, you know. I could help."

Peter laughed unpleasantly. "You? What could you do, pray tell? Can you plow? Can you drive a nail or deliver a calf? Sally, Sally, in the whole time at Water Garden, the hardest work I saw you do was tend to your sister-in-law's baby."

She flushed, stung by what was, after all, only the truth. "I suppose la Belle Annabella is skilled in all the farming arts?" she asked sarcastically. "If laying about all day moping and reading those dreadful novels from the Minerva Press, waiting for time to change for dinner and flirt with whatever man is available is farm work, than I suppose she is a true Mrs. Goodwife."

"She was brought up here. She loves Marchman Place as I do," Peter replied hotly.

Sally straightened her spine. Her back ached from the tension of the evening. "Yes, then I suppose she does," she agreed.

"Relations arguing, arguing, arguing." Peter yawned, stretching in the doorway. One of his black silk stockings slipped loose from his corbeau evening breeches and fell about his ankle, unnoticed. "I don't think you'd want to live in the Dower House anyway," he added sleepily. "Full of rats last time I looked. A cousin used to live there. Great-Aunt Aurelia's generation. Kept peacocks. Shrieked like souls in hell. Gervais and I used to pot at them with slingshots. It made them bloody angry, lemme tell you." He scratched at his chest through his shirt, yawning again. "Anyway, all Marchmans fight with each other like cats and dogs. Should have been here when m' grandfather, m' uncle, and m' father were all alive. Dreadful rows, over nothing. Aunts and female cousins just as bad, always ruffled up about something. Lord, it was dreadful. Gran'father tried to kill m' uncle at the dinner table one night with a fruit knife. Fishguard had to pull 'em apart. Something about a horse, as I recall. Or was it William Pitt? Maybe it was William Pitt's horse." He yawned again, this time very widely. "Come to bed, Sally, been a long day."

As he spoke, he turned and left the room, without looking at her where she sat huddled and pensive on the chaise.

After he had blown the candle out, she lay down on the chaise, pulling the thin cashmere counterpane up around her neck, her eyes wide open as she stared into the darkness, pondering.

12

Only select members of the household staff
were there to witness Lady Aurelia's departure
from Marchman Place the following morning.

"Don't bother to wake 'em up," she instructed
Fishguard as she climbed, with some difficulty
and the assistance of her outrider, into her enormous and elaborate traveling carriage. Attired
for her journey in sensible taupe carriage capes,
a mauve turban of several magnificent plumes
covering her silver locks, she was content to settle easily back against the blue silk squabs, her
gloved hands clutching her reticule, as her maid,
Fishguard, the housekeeper, and the first footman variously fluffed up her carriage cushions,
put a hot brick beneath her feet, spread a light
summer robe over her lap, loaded a wicker basket of such necessities as a crock of India tea,
macaroons baked special for her by Cook, a cold
lobster, a loaf of bread, strawberries from the
home farm, clotted cream from the dairy, and a
bottle of the very best brandy, should she feel
the need of a restorative. Since, save for Charles
the footman, most of these servants were no more
than a decade her junior, she privately amused
herself at their concern for her comfort, treating
her as if she were so fragile she must be wrapped
in cotton wool. A little ague and old age were all

that bothered her, but aloud she was gracious and appreciative in a way that might have astonished certain members of her family.

"I do, again, thank you all," she said as Fishguard and the housekeeper, satisfied that she would meet with no mishaps upon her journey to London, dismounted from the carriage. "And I do ask you, my old friends," she added, squeezing their hands and looking into their eyes, "to keep an eye upon that girl. The pair of them, knowing nothing more about how to go on than a moonling, have a rough road ahead. But you and I, we recall what Marchman Place was like in its glory, and perhaps with your help, they can bring it all around again, the way it should be."

Fishguard and the housekeeper nodded; that lady was seen to dab at a corner of her eye with her apron. "Now, you remember to eat up that chicken-foot jelly, my lady," she said. "Good for the lumbago."

With a bow, Fishguard closed the door, signaling the coachman. With a rumble of yellow wheels, the stately old coach swayed down the long drive past the ancient yew trees.

"Now, there's a lady and no mistake," Fishguard said. "Not like some I could mention, and always a pleasure to do for, ever since she was but a slip of a girl in the schoolroom."

Within the coach, Lady Aurelia sighed, settling her rather rotund figure comfortably into the seat. Or as comfortably as she could, for even a coach as large, luxurious, and well-sprung as hers was not precisely like riding upon a cloud, particularly on the rough and rutted roads of Devon.

"Well, Hurlock," she said to her abigail, a woman of nearly her own age who was as tall and thin as she was short and stout. "That's over and done with, but still and all, I cannot help but have a feeling that we still have a part to play in this little farce." Lady Aurelia loved the theater.

Miss Hurlock, as gray, dour, and majestic as the lady she had worked for these past forty-five years, settled her bony frame into her seat and put her spectacles upon her long nose. "Let us hope, my lady," she said in her slow, deliberate voice, "that that is merely one of your fancies. Should you wish me to read aloud to you? We were halfway through Northanger Abbey on the way up from town."

Lady Aurelia dug into her reticule and withdrew a small ivory-handled pistol. "Must be certain it's loaded," she said, squinting at it as she pointed it out the window.

Miss Hurlock sighed, looking rather severely over her glasses at her mistress. "My lady, the last highwayman on the Honiton Road was hung twenty years ago," she reminded her repressively.

Lady Aurelia's plumes nodded as she shook her head. "I know that. We went to see him turned off, recall? Black Jack Poolstock, it was. Made a very pretty speech before they opened the trap. No, Lord Robert always commanded me to carry my pistol whenever I ventured out of London, and so I do. Old habits die— Hello, what's that? Hurlock, have John Coachman stop at once."

Hurlock did as she was bid, craning her neck to follow Lady Aurelia's line of vision out the window. At first, all she saw was a fine June day in a green countryside, but in a second, she perceived a figure in a cardinal, bearing a bandbox under one arm, wearily trudging along the hedgerow.

"Just a farm girl, my lady," she said.

"I rather think not. Hurlock, open the door, if you please," Lady Aurelia commanded, digging into her reticule to produce her own pair of spectacles. Placing them on her nose, she let up the window and thrust her head, plumes and all, out into the air. "Well, gel, and just what do you think you might be doing?" she demanded imperiously.

"Lady Marchman!" Miss Hurlock was compelled to exclaim in deeply shocked tones, for, indeed, the weary figure in the scarlet cloak and (Hurlock noted with a professional eye) the sadly crushed sprig muslin was no farm girl, but Baroness Marchman herself, hot, perspiring, and decidedly showing signs of having indulged in a prolonged bout of weeping as she stopped beside the coach and looked up at the two elderly females inside, from one to the other.

"I'm going home," Lady Marchman announced, using the hand that held the bandbox to wipe ineffectually at her swollen eyes.

"By home, I shall assume that you mean the United States, gel?" Lady Aurelia asked, concealing a tiny smile.

Sally nodded. "I want to go home!" She wailed suddenly and burst into tears. "I want my mother and my father and my brothers. I want Water Garden."

"Oh, dear me," murmured Miss Hurlock as much at the potential scandal as at Sally's distress.

"Unless I am very much mistaken, dear gel, only divine persons can walk upon the water, even an ocean so rough as the Atlantic. Are you, by any chance, divine?" Lady Aurelia inquired reasonably. Years of being an aunt had given her a certain tolerance for the foibles of children, even children of one and twenty and married to scapegrace nephews who were Going to Hear About This.

"Of course not," Sally exclaimed irritably, not at all amused. She set down her bandbox and produced a rather soggy handkerchief.

"Please, use mine," Lady Aurelia said quickly, digging into her reticule and producing a tiny square of lacy cambric that she handed down to Sally, who used it to blow her nose.

"Really, my lady," Hurlock murmured, "a public thoroughfare—"

It had occurred to Lady Aurelia to point out to Lady Marchman the total impropriety of a baroness, even a baroness in a shabby red cardinal walking alone and unescorted on a major road used by every manner of person, including highwaymen, gypsies, and even less savory types, but she wisely decided that such an observation would put Lady Marchman even further into the role of a Tragedy Jill, and that was a scene she wished to avoid at all costs. Besides, she had taken one of her fancies to Peter's wife, and when she fancied a person, they could do no serious wrong. Therefore, she made a small gesture to Miss Hurlock and waited for Sally to finish blowing her nose and wiping at her eyes.

"No, ma'am," Sally said at last, in tones of utter misery. "I shall make for Plymouth and take ship there for home." She raised her chin slightly. "Once I am home, I am sure that my father will make all the necessary arrangements for the divorce. The colonel," she added woefully, "is a great believer in making your bed and lying in it, but I am certain that when he finds how shabbily I have been used, he will consent to it. And I wish that conniving chit well of him. Let her see how she likes his snoring, and his habit of picking his teeth with a penknife in bed while he reads— And I should like, above all things, to see her plow a field or birth a calf. She certainly has no notion of holding household."

While the two females in the carriage tried to sort out this speech, Sally looked very much as if she were about to launch into another flood of tears. "Oh," she exclaimed, "if only I could keep my wretched temper under check! I know they are your family, ma'am, but such things I do not feel I should have to endure, even if he thinks it perfectly all right to stab your son with a fruit knife."

"They are my family, and a dashed pack of fly-by-nights, loose screws, and mooncalves they are," Lady Aurelia agreed easily. "Well, gel, you can chose your friends, but you can't chose your family, so you mustn't blame me! I can, however, chose my friends, and so I have chosen you, gel. Don't tell me you intend to walk all the way to Plymouth."

Sally shrugged. "I hadn't thought about it," she confessed. "I thought and thought and thought all night, and I got angrier and angrier and angrier, and at dawn, I knew the only thing I could do was leave. I have nowhere to go but back home, you see, and I can't stay here. No one likes Americans," she added gloomily.

"We do, don't we, Hurlock?" Aunt Aurelia asked. "I recall that handsome Mr. Jefferson when he was in London. If I'd been twenty years younger, I should have beat out that insipid Maria Cosway ..." Her voice took on a reminiscent quality, and Miss Hurlock cleared her throat, recalling Lady Aurelia to herself. "Yes, where were we? Oh, Plymouth. It's hundred and hundreds of miles away, you know. But you could go by post, if you had the money."

"How much?" Sally asked doubtfully. Clearly, money was something she had forgotten to bring along.

"Oh, I should say a good hundred guineas," Lady Aurelia replied airily. "And of course, you'd have to tip the postboy, and the ostlers, and you'd lie on the road two nights, that's another five or eight pounds for a decent hotel—that is, if they'd put you up unaccompanied by man or maid, which I don't see being likely, not in the sort of place you would want to sleep with your own room, rather than three strangers to a bed."

"And then, there's the passage money," John Coachman added his mite from the box. Like all of Lady Aurelia's staff, he had been with her for a goodly number of years.

"That's another hundred pounds and not even a private cabin," Sally calculated gloomily.

"And of course, you'll have to stay at Plymouth, waiting for a ship to America. That could take days or months. And even then, the first one leaving might not be going to where you want to go, and you'd have to make your way from Boston or Savannah or Santo Domingo."

Sally looked quite frightened, which was the desired result. Now, Lady Aurelia thought, she knew how simple it was for unscrupulous persons of the sort one read about in the lesser newspapers to kidnap young girls. "If you please," she said in her tyrannical voice, "do not make yourself into a watering pot, my gel. Obviously, as I shall tell Vicar when next I see him, Providence, in one of its rare sensible gestures, has placed us here to rescue you from a great deal of unnecessary unpleasantness."

"I don't care if I'm raped and killed," Sally said with a flash of her old self, "I'm *not* going back there!"

"Neither am I," Aunt Aurelia agreed. "A thoroughly depressing lot of people. *I* am going to my house near Grosvenor Square, where there are no extremely tiresome relatives to put me into a taking, and I can have everything ordered just as I like it. Well, of course, there is Gervais, who does drop by from time to time, but he's so delightful, one can hardly consider him a relation."

"I wish I could see Gervais," Sally said wistfully. "I did like him, and I want to tell him good-bye."

"Well, then, enough of this shilly-shallying about and crying over spilt milk and spoiled beauties," Lady Aurelia exclaimed, growing a trifle bored. "It would seem to me, my gel, that the best thing for you to do would be to come to London with me and have a taste of town bronzing. Might as well see all the sights and lions before you go home. When you are at my house, you may write your papa a letter and explain the circumstances to him, and see what he thinks best."

Sally clutched her bandbox, shaking her head. "I couldn't impose," she said firmly. "It wouldn't be proper at all."

"My dear gel, if you do not have yourself in this carriage in thirty seconds, I shall have the outrider place you in here by force," Lady Aurelia commanded imperiously. "And I warn you, I brook no interference when I have decided upon a course."

Sally grinned, pushing her hair out of her face. "Yes, ma'am," she said meekly, and climbed in.

"Hurlock, tell John Coachman we may go on," Lady Aurelia said, reaching into the wicker basket. "I think we could all do with a smidgeon of Fishguard's excellent French brandy, which I wager pays no excise tax. Then, my dear Sarah, you may tell us what events transpired to put you into *such* a taking."

By the time they were approaching Salisbury, where Lady Aurelia made it her custom to lie at the Four Swans to break the long journey between London and Marchman Place, the contents of the bottle of brandy seemed to have mysteriously disappeared in direct proportion to the rising tide of optimism felt by all three ladies.

Having agreed that Lord Marchman was sadly lacking in both sensibility and sense, and a monstrous husband of Gothic proportions, neglectful and without consideration for the tender feelings of his new bride, a female of such grace, manners, and warmth that his indifference surpassed all understanding, they had gone on to ruthlessly dissect the character of Annabella. Miss Hurlock opined that after forty-five years in service, she knew her place, but would venture to say that during her interrupted London Season, Miss Annabella had not precisely endeared herself to belowstairs at Upper Mount Street. Lady Aurelia responded that she had done very little to endear herself abovestairs, either, and that from the cradle, the beauty had been spoiled and cosseted by all of her unfortunate male relations, which inevitably led to the character of Mrs. Theresa Marchman being raked over the coals in a merciless fashion. It was generally agreed that her die-away airs and aura of false martyrdom were a very thin concealment of a nature as selfish as it was lazy, and that her total inability to impart even the most basic precepts of propriety and conduct upon her daughter displayed a deplorable lack of maternal instinct.

Having shredded the character of these three persons into minute bits, the ladies felt much better and were able to accept the obsequious hospitality of the landlord and lady of the Four Swans as their just due for so exhausting a day upon the road. If the hostlers of this establishment, which catered only to the quality, were astonished that such an august personage as Lady Aurelia should have in tow a rather rumpled-looking miss with only one bandbox to her name, they were far too discreet to give evidence of it, accepting Lady Marchman's odd appearance as if it were an everyday occurrence.

Too tired to care what anyone thought of her, Sally put away an excellent dinner of roast lamb, fresh peas, fried lettuce, and mulled cider in Lady Aurelia's private parlor, while that female watched her new charge from beneath her hooded hawklike eyes, a faint, amused smile playing over her lips as she toyed, with less appetite, at her own plate. Precisely what amused her was not clear, but as she spooned at her sherry trifle, listening to Sally's exclamations of delight over her first dessert of strawberries with clotted Devonshire cream, she cleared her throat slowly.

Sally looked up at her expectantly. Really, Lady Aurelia thought, the American chit was no beauty, those freckles were deplorable, that sandy hair not in style (oh, that powder had not gone out of fashion!), but she was not a quiz, either. She had very nice eyes and quite a pretty little mouth, and her figure, while slightly full, was attractive. But what set her apart were her unique qualities. That drawling accent could be qute delightful, for instance, and she was intelligent and well-spoken, with an unconsciously devastating honesty that Lady Aurelia found quite refreshing after Season after Season of undereducated, simpering, man-hungry debutantes. Of course Sarah was no deb, but a married lady, and a baroness at that. That great gawk fool Peter! She could cheerfully wring his stupid, charming neck. If he had had the least particle of sense, he would have sent Theresa and Annabella packing—to a hired house in London for the Season, or to, better yet, Bath. Just like his father and uncle and grandfather, she thought wearily. But that, for the moment, did not solve the problem of Sarah, and, she thought, Sarah was going to be a problem, if she moped about Upper Mount Street, blue-deviled over a fight with Peter. Annabella! Really!

Suddenly, Sally clapped her hands to her cheeks. "I forgot to leave him a letter," she exclaimed. "Now he'll wonder where I am. He might be out searching the caves and the crags, looking for me, when he should be putting the south acres into grazing clover."

It was upon the tip of Lady Aurelia's tongue to suggest a message be dispatched to Marchman Place by ostler, but some instinct immediately repressed the thought, for good or bad. Rather, she said aloud, "Let him search. It will do him good to stew in his own juices after the cake he made of himself last night, my gel."

Sally looked doubtful. "However I feel about it, it would be dreadfully cruel not to let him know that I'm with you and quite safe."

"Probably so," Lady Aurelia agreed dryly, folding her small hands across her round waist. "But, my gel, if you intend to divorce him, as you say, then what possible difference can it make?"

Sally looked at her dish, biting her lower lip. "I spoke in temper, ma'am," she said softly. "Oh, my stupid, wretched temper!"

"Well, I still hold that it is not entirely your fault, Sarah. Peter has behaved in a very ramshackle fashion. *All* the Marchman men do, you know! Of course, they never mean harm, but what devastation they wreak!" She examined the lavaliere about her neck. "Of course, leaving him with Annabella in such a fashion, you know, is leaving the cat among the pigeons."

"Perhaps I ought to go back," Sally said, looking as if she meant to push away from the table and make her departure at that moment.

"No, my dear gel, I rather think not. In the war between men and women, no one ever won by reentering the scene of a lost battle." It sounded profound, Lady Aurelia thought. She hoped Sally found it so. "No, I think what we shall do is make him come to you."

Sally's eyebrows rose. "But how can he, when he doesn't even know where I am?" she asked reasonably.

"He'll know when the time comes," Lady Aurelia replied mysteriously. "Well, my dear gel, I am off to bed. So exhausting, travel. We shall work it all out tomorrow."

Sally hoped this was true. For some reason she had placed all her faith with Lady Aurelia.

13

The last leg of the journey was accomplished in a slightly more mundane fashion. While Hurlock read aloud from Miss Austen's new novel, *Northanger Abbey*, a thoughtfully silent Lady Aurelia concealed her pensive mood by playing several games of chess with Sally upon an ebony and ivory traveling board. Sally was a credible opponent who could give the dowager a good game, and by the time they arrived in Upper Mount Street, just before midnight, Lady Aurelia was inclined to be quite in charity with her houseguest.

For her part, Sally, never having seen a metropolis quite so large and bustling as London, was quite fascinated and had to be reminded several times to keep from thrusting her head out the window at every sight, and concentrate on the board. She had never seen the likes of the gaslights, installed the previous year, and rather naïvely exclaimed over the ability of this new and miraculous invention to illuminate the better parts of town through which they traveled.

Indeed, it was not until Lady Aurelia's housekeeper led her up the stairs to her own room, a charmingly feminine bedchamber done in Queen Anne and eau de Nile, ascertained that she did not require anything further that evening, and

151

left her to herself, that Sally sat down in the wing chair and drew her knees up to her chin, gazing out the window and wondering what Peter was doing, and what she herself was doing in a strange house in London, all alone and rather afraid.

The previous night, she had found it hard to sleep without the pressure of his back against her own, and the rhythm of his snoring to lull her into dreams. She wondered if he missed her, and if he had trouble sleeping. Or was he simply relieved that she had removed herself from his life, solving his problem in a tidy manner?

At that moment, she did not feel at all like a married woman, but very much like a frightened child, glad that the gaslights burned all night, softly illuminating this strange room.

As she was finally drifting off to sleep, the thought passed through her mind that this would all be so much more fun if he were here. . . .

In the morning, a maid brought a tray into her room, tsking slightly that she had left the windows open against the unhealthy night air, and all agog with a barely suppressed curiosity to see the American Lady Marchman. Slightly disappointed that Sally was not a red Indian, but merely a young woman with strawberry hair and a rather sad smile whose most unusual characteristic was a preference for coffee over tea with her toast, the little maid bobbed a curtsy, and in an accent as difficult for Sally to comprehend as her own Maryland drawl was for this cockney chit, ascertained that my lady needed no assistance in dressing, informed her that Lady Aurelia wished to see her in her writing room as soon as was convenient, and departed to pick all of this over with the rest of the maids.

When she had attired herself in an ivory muslin morning dress pressed out by Hurlock, Sally wandered about the splendors of Lady Aurelia's rather modest Queen Anne town house until she located the writing room at the back of the house. Sunlight poured through the windows overlooking the tiny garden, and Lady Aurelia, in a lacy mob cap tied beneath her several chins and a robe de chambre of Brussels lace, sat at a delicate Louis XVI desk, its entire top seemingly covered with correspondence.

"Ah," she said briskly, "there you are, my gel. I've sent a footman around to the Albany after Gervais, so I daresay he'll be along around eleven. It takes him two hours to dress, you know."

Sally did not know, but she could believe it. "I should like to see Gervais," she said as Lady Aurelia gestured her into a spindly gilt chair.

"You sit there. I certainly couldn't, since I put on seventeen stone," she said frankly, playing with the nib of her pen as she studied Sally thoughtfully. "Well, my dear gel, I have decided," she announced. It was a message from Olympus. "I think, first of all, that it would be a very good thing if you were to have some new clothes. After all, gel, you can't go about London in two rumpled dresses and a cardinal out of a bandbox, can you?"

Sally shook her head. "I suppose not," she admitted, unconsciously smoothing out the ribands of her belt.

Lady Aurelia nodded. She did not expect to be disagreed with. "So, I have decided that Gervais, whose taste in female fashion, if not waistcoats, is impeccable, shall take you to Madame Céleste. She's quite fashionable and very dear, but don't worry about the money. Peter can stand the brass."

Sally smiled.

"That's more like, my gel," Lady Aurelia said briskly. "So, my dear, when you're all rigged out as fine as a fivepence," Lady Aurelia continued in her Georgian way, "you'll have to go somewhere to be seen in your new finery, my gel. Vouchers to Almack's are no problem. A very dull sort of place, but deadly fashionable and quite respectable." She looked down at the mass of correspondence on her desk as if it had suddenly appeared from nowhere, demanding her attention. "Where do they all come from?" she wondered. "I really can't know them all, can I? Out of town for a fortnight, and how it all piles up, even for a widow living alone."

She sighed, glancing above the desk at a kit-cat of a gentleman Sally presumed to be the late Sir Robert. "Well, I shall sift through all of it and choose the parties that I think you will enjoy. Mind you, my gel, no fast company, none of that Petersham set or any of that, although it is a great shame about poor Byron. Quite beyond the pale, of course, but I think you would have enjoyed him. Well, we shall see. A rather nice set of young people, I think, nothing too fast, but not too slow either. Won't have myself fagged to death by bluestockings."

Completely at a loss, Sally merely listened.

"Ah," Lady Aurelia said after a moment's perusal of the invitations. "Kean's doing his Hamlet tonight. I thought that would be amusing. Personally, I can't abide this naturalistic school of acting. It's a great pity that dear Sarah Siddons retired from the stage to live in Bath, of all places! But we shall gird our loins and go to see Edmund Kean chew the scenery tonight."

"Theater!" Sally said with considerably more enthusiasm than she had shown for Almack's or fashionable parties. "Oh, yes, I should love to go to the theater above all things. All I have ever seen have been traveling players, and once, Father took us all to see a play when we were in Philadelphia. It was a turgid melodrama of the *worst* sort, but I assure you, I was enthralled."

"I hope you will not be like every silly goose in the city and fall in love with Kean," Lady Aurelia remarked, writing something on a missive. "He's quite mad, you know. All artists are. That's why one doesn't invite them to dinner. They throw food. Except, of course, dear Sarah. A perfect lady." Thus spoke the voice of experience.

Fascinated, Sally stored this away for future reference. Not that she expected to meet any artists, at least not under Aunt Aurelia's roof, but one never did know.

"I think I am more mad with the prospect of seeing Shakespeare actually performed upon a stage by actors than I could ever be over this Mr. Kean," Sally said thoughtfully. And anyway, she thought, how could I lose my heart to an actor when it already lies with Peter? She felt a twinge of sadness, picturing him all alone, wandering over the fields, yearning for her. More likely, she told herself sternly, he was sharing a picnic lunch with Annabella.

"And music, of course. You did say that you liked music, did you not, Sarah?" Lady Aurelia asked abruptly, as if she had read Sally's thoughts and desired to steer them into happier channels.

"Oh, yes, above all things, I do like music,"

Sally exclaimed. "I play myself, you know. The pianoforte."

Then, why in heaven's name, child, Lady Aurelia thought, scratching her numerous chins with the quill as she glanced over the Academy program, did you not get up and upstage that silly chit with a superior performance? That is what I would have done. Poor thing, you wish to present yourself to the world as cool and self-possessed, when underneath, your feelings bubble like boiling water. If someone had tried to steal Lord Robert from me, I should have fought with every weapon I had at my disposal. She smiled, recalling the times she had done just that. Lady Aurelia, having been born formidable, often had trouble understanding those of less commanding demeanor. She sighed to herself, positively enjoying this latest bit of meddling in other people's lives.

"Music," she said aloud, recalling herself to the present. "Yes. On Friday, there is a concert of Haydn at the Academy. I am very fond of music, myself, and subscribe to all the societies. Tell me, have you heard this new German, Beethoven?"

"Only of him," Sally said. "I tried to order his pianoforte pieces from New York, but in America, things take so long to reach us from Europe."

"Then we shall go to the society and hear his work. A symphony, I believe it says here. He is said to be quite a romantic composer. These romantics! Byron, Shelley, Keats, Turner, Constable, Beethoven! I confess that they are of a generation that I do not understand. It is a bad thing to get old and become too set in your ways, always wishing for the good old days." She smiled thinly at Sally, shaking her head. "The only thing that made them good was being young and naïve," she added briskly.

"Oh, ma'am," Sally said seriously, "I never think of you as old. Indeed, I think you are far more alive than Mrs. Marchman, who could probably give you thirty years!"

Lady Aurelia shook her head, amused. "I *think* I have been complimented," she murmured. "Careful, dear gel, I'm not one who likes flattery laid on with a trowel. Beethoven it is, then, next week!"

At that moment, the door of the writing room opened and the largest man Sally had ever seen in her life made a short bow in Lady Aurelia's direction. To judge from his livery, he was Duddle, the butler of which Lady Aurelia had spoken so fondly. But nothing her hostess had said had prepared Sally for the sight of a giant of a man who must stand six and a half feet tall in his stockings, and weigh as much as a large pony. His rather bulbous nose had evidently been broken at some distant date in the past, for it sported a very definite crook, precisely in the middle, while his eyebrows met right above this interesting proboscis in a very fierce sort of manner. His complexion was beefy, and his jaw large and square. Perched atop his big, square head was a small patch of hair so obviously of human manufacture that it resembled nothing so much as a small rug of a peculiar shade of blue black; beneath it, his pate gleamed fleshily and bald. His hands, properly encased in white cotton gloves, were the size of ham hocks, and when he opened his mouth to speak, a gold tooth gleamed disconcertingly bright among its white fellows.

"This," he said, in a basso-profundo voice with a friendly inflection and another barely comprehensible accent, "must be my lady Marchman, Mr. Peter's new bride."

Lady Aurelia inclined her head. "Lady Marchman, my butler, Duddle."

Duddle bent at the waist, and Sally wondered if he would be able to straighten up again. When he did, without apparent difficulty, she breathed more easily. "My lady, allow me to be presentin' you wid a small token of the respect and affection in which the hall holds the wife of Mr. Peter," he announced grandly in what Sally guessed to be a London accent of some sort. With a graceful flourish, surprising in such a large man, he produced a bouquet of violets.

As Sally took them from his huge hand, she smiled up at him and realized Duddle had made a friend and ally for life.

"There's some belowstairs," Duddle continued ominously, "who would have it that Mr. Peter came home from the Americas with a wild Indian for a wife, like that Pocahontas you read about, and was right disappointed when you didn't come callin' wearin' feathers an' skins and making to scalp Thomas. He's the second footman, my lady, you get it, and right skittish about being scalped, bein' that proud of a fine head of ginger hair. Well, some are mighty disappointed that you're a pretty young Christian lady. But I says, I says, Pearl, she bein' the upperhouse chambermaid, would you want to be waitin' on a wild Indian in beads and feathers and bear grease and whatnot to clean up instead of a nicely brought-up young lady what's fallen in love and married Mr. Peter under most romantic circumstances. *I* brought 'em around," he concluded, clearly proud of himself.

Sally could not help but burst out laughing,

the first time she had done so since she had left Maryland. Clutching the violets to her bosom, she threw back her head and went into peal after peal of merry laughter while Duddle and Lady Aurelia watched, amused. It took several seconds before she could hold out her hand, to have it clasped in that enormous, if quite gentle fist, and warmly shaken.

"T-thank you!" she said unsteadily. "Please— please t-thank everyone for me, and tell them that I am very sorry I'm only a strawberry blonde without so much as a drop of Cherokee blood in my veins, or a jot of bear grease to me name."

Duddle winked, nodding his head good-naturedly. "That I will tell them, miss. Mr. Peter is much liked belowstairs here, and has been ever since he was but a poppet in nappies, here wid his nurse. Speakin' for myself personal—and my lady can vouch for the fact that Albert Duddle never spoke a word that were not the truth, less'n, o' course, it were to say my lady ain't at home when she don't want to see some toad-eater or a dead bore . . ." He winked again, grinning at his employer. "Which is by way of bein' a white lie and not counting. Speaking for myself personal, as I was sayin', iffen there's anything at all you would be wanting, any errand or commission or message run or problem solved, all you 'ave to do is ask, just as my lady here does."

"T-thank you," Sally said, completely overwhelmed. "I—I am most grateful to you, Duddle."

"Well, Lady Marchman," Duddle said, looking her up and down with the eye of a judge, "you ain't no great beauty like Miss Annabella, but what I sez is beauty is as beauty does, and you're a right taking sort of mort, iffen you don't mind me saying so," he added, blithe in the assurance that she did not. "And should some o' these 'ere London bucks and rakehells and peep o'day boys and pinks of the fancy try to take advantage of the fact that you're from out of town, so to speak, and not well up on the ways of what goes for society here, all you need to do is call for me, and I'll land 'em a fiver that'll draw their corks from here to Temple Bar."

Sally laughed again. "No, I fear I am no diamond of the first water like Annabella, but I very much doubt that I shall be going anywhere where I shall meet any of the people you've described to me."

Duddle shook his great head so vehemently that his wig slipped slightly askew. Completely unabashed, he reached up and rearranged it again, still talking to Sally, who was hypnotized. "Mind now, miss—I mean, my lady! I was in the ring for a good many year before I went into service with Lord Robert, rest his soul, and my dearest Lady Aurelia here! They'd have to stick my spoon all the way into the wall before I'd let a soul harm a hair on her head, and I'll say the same offer for Mr. Peter's wife, too."

Vaguely beginning to comprehend that Duddle was a former boxer before he assumed his present occupation, and was offering her his services should any gentleman step out of bounds of propriety with her, Sally laughed a third time, but she was touched and grateful. "Thank you again, Duddle," she said sincerely, touching the sleeve of his coat lightly, gazing up at his gold tooth. "Should I ever require a knight-errant, I shall certainly not hesitate to call upon you."

Duddle nodded, satisfied. "With Mr. Peter not with you, someone's got to be your champeen," he announced stalwartly, crossing his enormous arms over his barrel of a chest and looking about the room as if he expected miscreants to appear out of the woodwork. "When will we see Mr. Peter in town?" he inquired, interested.

Sally bit her lip, looking down at her feet, too honest to tell even a white lie.

"Not for a while, Duddle," Lady Aurelia said soothingly. "He's got both hands full trying to pull the estate back into some semblance of shape, as well you may imagine."

Duddle nodded his massive head, drawing his thick black brows together like a caterpillar. "And so he must," he agreed sympathetically. "A right tangle the late lord, and the lord before him left it all in. Mr. Peter's got his work cut out for him." He smiled down at Sally. "So, miss, you've come to see all the sights? Astley's and whatnot?" he inquired in a more cheerful voice.

"I am afraid that I am so new to this country and this town that I do not even know what the sights might be," Sally confessed, back on safe ground again.

"Oh, now, miss! Dr. Samuel Johnson, he that used to come and see me box onc't in a while, said, you know, when a body's tired of London, he's tired of life! Meaning that there's that much to see and do. Why, I imagine we've got things here you never dreamed existed over in America."

"Such as?" Sally asked, enthralled by the spell of Duddle's personality. Just when you thought you couldn't get any more Duddle, he fooled you and did something so outlandish that you were simply fascinated, drawn into his magic against your will. He must have been wonderful when Peter and the rest were children, she thought, like having your own wizard.

"Such as?" Duddle's single brow traveled up

his pate. "Me being a Lunnder born and bred, it might be as how I could tell you what I would see, if I'd come to town to see the lions," he mused, rubbing his big square chin thoughtfully. "Well, I guess I'd go to Astley's and St. Paul's Cathedral and the Elgin Marbles, proper cultural they be, and—"

"What is Astley's?" Sally asked.

"Astley's Ampitheater? My hat, Lady Marchman, it's a circus. You go in and they have three great huge rings, and in each ring, there's some sort of act going on. Trained horses, bareback riders, people swinging through the air makin' all sort of fancy movement on trapezes, hundred of feet above your head, acting just as if they was on the swing in the old apple tree. They've got a female who rides bareback and does all manner of tricks and gymnastics on the back of a great white horse. Why, there's all kinds of marvels at Astley's. Used to take Mr. Peter and Mr. Gervais and Miss Annabella there when they was but poppets. Eyes got as big as saucers at all there was to see."

"If Peter loved it, then I shall have to go there too," Sally said, avoiding Lady Aurelia's long-suffering look. "Anyway, it sounds much more interesting than St. Paul's Cathedral or the Elgin Marbles," she added impishly.

Duddle agreed with her wholeheartedly, but pronounced it a great shame that under no circumstances would Lady Aurelia allow her to attend the masks at Covent Garden, which were, he opined, right interesting to watch, from a safe place, of course.

"Under no circumstances is Sarah—Lady Marchman to attend *any* of those lewd, wretched masks," Lady Aurelia announced firmly.

Duddle looked a little abashed. "Perhaps Lady Aurelia is right, my lady," he admitted sheepishly, scratching at his wig. "Hardly the sort of place where a lady would go, specially a young and inexperienced young lady like yourself, well-brought-up in America, where they don't have those things."

Sally was immediately intrigued, and resolved to pry all the details out of Duddle or Gervais at the first opportunity. Country-bred, her own town excursions into the burned-out capital of Washington, where little existed save L'Enfant's carefully designed government buildings, endless stretches of Chesapeake marsh and shabby boardinghouses where senators and ambassadors shuffled by on dirty sheets and indifferent food, meant that the idea of something naughty and scandalous and sophisticated—not to mention forbidden—intrigued her no end. If only the very fastest of the fashionable went to these affairs, they must be more her image of vague and book-learned ideas of European decadence than the rather dreary and uncomfortable dinner parties Lady Aurelia suggested. "When Lady Aurelia is not about, you shall tell me all the details," she teased Duddle. "Or if you will not, I am certain my cousin Gervais will do so."

A look of great pain crossed Duddle's beefy countenance, and he slapped an enormous hand against his forehead. "What am I thinking of?" he demanded. "I *am* sorry, my lady, but in all the excitement of makin' the acquaintance of Mr. Peter's new lady-wife, it dropped out of my mind that I was supposed to announce that Mr. Gervais is sittin' in the blue study, coolin' his boots. And a fine pair of shiny, tasseled Hessians they are, too," he added seriously.

"My dear man," drawled a familiar voice from the doorway, "if my aunt continues to retain you as a butler for any other purpose than sheer amusement value, I have failed to see what it might be. Just look what you've made me do. I had to sit on that wretched Jacobite settle for a full fifteen minutes, twiddling my thumbs, and it has quite ruined the press of my coattails."

Duddle hung his head. "I am sorry, Mr. Gervais," he said meekly. "Iffen you would wish me to take your coat and press it—"

Gervais threw up a hand, gloved in lemon yellow, in horror. "God forbid," he exclaimed, not quite irreverently. "If my valet discovered I had as much as allowed someone else to *look* at this coat, he would leave me for Alvaney. And we *cannot* have that happen. Wrinkled it will have to remain, as I have a strong premonition that it will be even more depressingly wrinkled before the end of this day. Aunt never summons me at the crack of vampire dawn unless she has some particularly gruesome emergency project for me to deal with for her. Why I do so, I do not know, unless it is that she is as depressingly tonnish as I am. Certainly, it could not be any ties of family affection, for none of the Marchmans can abide any of the others. Hullo, what's this?"

Gervais lifted an ornate gold quizzing glass to his eye, magnifying this orb into hideous distortion as he surveyed Sally from head to toe. "Madame Céleste's," he announced, dropping the glass on its riband about his neck. "At once. Good Lord, girl, where did you get that fright of a dress, from some old clothes dealer specializing in girl's boarding-school cast-offs? Come now, we *are* Lady Marchman, are we not? Or are we? I fail to percieve the vague odor of sulfur and brimstone that always seems to surround my dear cousin.''

Sally, rendered temporarily nonplussed by Gervais' theatrical entrance, was torn between the urge to hug him and deliver him a strong setdown concerning her dress. But she found that all she could do was simply sit and take in the awful magnificence of his haberdashery, the very zenith of male fashion, at least at that moment. He was indeed wearing a pair of Hessian boots polished to a mirrored shine, and adorned with golden tassels and scarlet tops. From these examples of elegant footwear, a pair of buckskin breeches traveled up his thighs toward his waistcoat, so tightly molded to his form that she suspected his valet had sewn him into them only minutes before. His waistcoat was an intriguing stripe of Charlotte blue and buff, done up in a watered silk. From his large, heavy-linked gold watch chain there dangled a single pyramid-shaped fob, set with a pearl the size of a robin's egg, while his coat, a bath superfine done in a darker shade of Charlotte blue, sported a pair of tufted ruches nearly four inches high, and precisely on parallel with the high stock of his cravat, an affair so starched and pointed that it threatened to scrape his ears should he turn his head in either direction. His neckcloth was a masterpiece that even a naïve like Sally could recognize as having come from the hand of a master. It dipped and folded and rippled about his stock in a shape that vaguely resembled, when taken with the precise and tiny knot used to fasten it, a sort of odd-looking bird. In one hand, he carried a malacca cane, tipped at head and foot with ornate gold castings of something that looked vaguely pornographic to Sally, while in the other, he delicately held between thumb and forefinger, a pearl-gray beaver hat with quite the deepest crown she had ever seen. It made perfect sense that its hat band was the same watered silk as the waistcoat, although why this should be so, Sally was uncertain. Indeed, she was not entirely certain that Gervais did not look rather foolish in his ensemble, but decided that since he had made the wearing of clothing his life's occupation, he was entitled to be considered in the first stare of fashion.

Having paused just long enough in the doorway to allow his relations to admire him, Gervais broke his pose and gave Sally a broad, lazy smile. "My dear coz, I would embrace you, of course, but I fear that it would rumple my neckcloth, so a kiss upon your hand will have to do." He bent, with a suspicious creaking sound, over Sally's hand, planting a dry, ironic kiss upon it before moving lazily toward his aunt.

"You will forgive me for greeting Cousin Sally first, dear Aunt," he drawled, bending over her hand. "But she was closer, you see, and with the horrible blue devils one has this morning, one tries to do everything in the simplest possible way."

"Drinkin blue ruin in one o' them boozin' kens again?" Duddle asked knowledgeably.

Gervais threw him a filthy look. "Duddle, whyn't you toddle off and polish the silver or whatever it is you do about here? And, for your information, it was a cockfight, and, yes, I lost an obscene amount of money."

Duddle chuckled as he went out the door.

Very gently, Gervais eased himself into a fragile-looking gilt and blue armchair, crossing one Hessian over the other and pressing his fingers against his forehead. "I do hope that Duddle is going to have mercy on me and fix one of his gentle concoctions before I have to go and do whatever it is that I have to go and do today. I take it that this somehow involves our dear Cousin Sally?" He glanced from Lady Aurelia to Sally, looking rather sullen, but not entirely unwilling to be persuaded if the task were interesting enough. His life had been dull enough lately to send him into one of his lumming expeditions, a diversion he invariably came to regret the next day.

"Sarah's left Peter," Lady Aurelia said, not mincing words.

"Do tell," Gervais responded conversationally, smiling at Sally.

Lady Aurelia nodded. "What it's all about, don't signify. Suffice to say that Peter's acted like, well, just as one would expect a Marchman male to act, and Sally's come to stay with me for a while."

Gervais' eyes glittered, and a little smile turned up the corners of his lips as he looked at Sally. "Do *tell*," he purred.

"So," Lady Aurelia went on, her voice deceptively casual, "you and I, my dear boy, will simply have to make her fashionable. Can't have her staying with me and not being fashionable. It wouldn't do."

"I think that I might scent the faintest trace of one of your managing schemes, Aunt," the dandy remarked, withdrawing a porcelain snuffbox from a pocket and proceeding to inhale deeply.

"F-fashionable?" Sally suddenly spoke up. "But I don't think that I wish to be fashionable."

"Of course you do, my dear coz. *Everyone* does. Besides, it's highly diverting, once you get the hang of the thing. Of course, one may become too fashionable and have to rusticate for a while, until it all passes over, but I don't think we need worry about that with you, coz. If I may say so, you are depressingly proper.''

Sally was unsure of what to make of the look he gave her, or the hidden meaning behind the light, bantering tone of his voice. She cut her eyes at him. ''Perhaps I don't wish to be depressingly proper anymore,'' she said a little haughtily. ''What's sauce for the goose is sauce for the gander.''

''I do like to see you entering into the spirit of things,'' Gervais remarked. ''Well, Aunt, I do agree with you that she must be presented to society. After all, Sally is Lady Marchman. Lord, family obligations!'' He shook his pomaded locks and smiled brightly. ''This, however, ought to be great fun, don't you think? Be fun to see our Sally up to every rig and row in town.''

''Not quite *every* rig and row in town,'' Lady Aurelia said meaningfully, with a strong look at her nephew.

Gervais nodded. ''No, not quite every, not for our Sally,'' he brooded thoughtfully, tilting the delicate chair back on its legs in a most precarious fashion and propping his chin with the head of his cane. ''Howsoever, dear coz, I do not see that a little town bronzing is going to destroy whatever precarious situation you and Peter have placed yourselves in. In fact, it may help a great deal, one way or the other.''

''This is all quite above my head,'' Sally admitted.

''Exactly so! And that is why you need to be on the town, dear coz,'' Gervais announced, bringing the chair down with a sharp bang that made Lady Aurelia close her eyes and wince for her antiques. "Come, my little coz, your fairy godparents are about to make Cinderella ready for the ball." He held out his hand toward Sally, and she took it, allowing him to pull her up from her seat.

At that moment, Duddle entered the room, bearing a vile-appearing potion on a silver tray. Without missing a beat, Gervais lifted the glass to his lips and drank. By the time he and Sally were out the door, he had drained the glass.

"Thank you, my good man," he said, handing it to a startled footman. "Come, Cinderella, your carriage awaits. We must make haste, lest you turn into a pumpkin."

Half-amused, half-trusting, Sally took her chipstraw hat from the maid and placed it firmly upon her head.

14

"I must say, coz, I am extremely grateful to Auntie for lending us her barouche for this excursion into the darkest world of women's garments. It would never do for me to be seen driving you about in my phaeton wearing that quiz of a hat," Gervais remarked lightly. "Thank the Lord for Duddle's little talents. I rather used to believe that Aunt kept him on as a conversation piece, but every time I encounter him, I find yet another indispensable talent he possesses. My blue devils have quite evaporated."

"What's wrong with my hat?" Sally demanded, a trifle incensed. She tilted it at a more rakish angle over her eyes.

"What's not wrong with it?" Gervais retorted. "My dear coz, you are not Miss, ah, Goldsborough, living on some backwater plantation anymore. You are Lady Marchman, a peeress and a member of the upper ten thousand, and it's about time you began to dress the part." Playfully, Gervais pulled the little chipstraw hat down over her eyes.

"Stop it, or I shall ruin that silly cravat," Sally threatened, laughing. "Anyway, I may not be Lady Marchman for very much longer," she added in a more somber tone.

Gervais whistled through his teeth, a most undandylike thing to do. "Annabella up to her usual tricks, then?" he asked in a gentler tone.

Miserably, Sally nodded.

"That is an old sad story," Gervais mused. "You do know, of course, that Peter doesn't love her, never has, never will?"

Sally picked at her cotton gloves, noting a smudge on one finger. "I know nothing of the kind. Oh, we had a row, and it was dreadful and we both said a great many unkind things to each other and—"

"Here now, don't cry all over me. Ruin my waistcoat. Won't do! No female who's going out to have thousands of pounds' worth of clothes bought for her should be in tears."

Sally tried to smile. Very gently, Gervais took her hand into his own, holding it firmly in his lap. She was barely aware that one elegantly tailored arm had slid, at some cost to his coat, about her shoulders, but she did know that it felt very good to be held. "D-dear Gervais," she managed to say.

He laughed, a little cynically. "Dear Cousin Gervais! Yes, I do think so, you know, Sally. Poor stupid Annabella, she's vain and foolish and utterly wretched at plotting and scheming— even when we were children, I could read through her machinations like tissue paper, but still—"

The thought formed in the back of Sally's mind that Gervais might have formed a *tendre* for Annabella, but preoccupied with her own problems, she allowed it to slip past her unheeded. "Only let me tell you what sort of a low, underhanded piece of jobbery she pulled on me," Sally said bitterly, and proceeded to describe the experience to Gervais.

Instead of being sympathetic and angry, as she had hoped he would be, he merely laughed. "A very good joke," he exclaimed. "And precisely the sort of obvious, mutton-headed entanglement that a green 'un like you would fall for."

"I am *not* a green 'un," Sally sputtered indignantly.

"Yes you are, Cousin Sally, but before either of us is much older, you won't be a green 'un anymore," Gervais promised gaily. "Lord, but Annabella makes a wretched, amateurish villainess." He laughed.

"Simple enough for you to say," Sally retorted. "She has not tried to lure your husband away from you, nor made your life miserable."

"The former, no; the latter, yes, many times, and more than I care to admit to," Gervais pronounced, a trifle enigmatically.

Sally came out of herself just enough to start to pursue this thought, studying Gervais' handsome profile curiously, but at that moment the barouche came to a halt and the footman pulled down the trap.

"Here we are, dear coz. Madame Céleste's. Don't allow yourself to be overwhelmed, or you shall be eaten alive by the old harpy," he added with a wink.

It did not occur to Sally to wonder why Madame Céleste, a hawk-nosed Frenchwoman of an indeterminate age, should personally emerge from the back of her very elegant salon to greet Gervais as an old and valued customer, when Gervais was a bachelor with no sisters or mother to make claims upon his attentions to female dress.

If she had known that Gervais had outfitted a long and diverse series of mistresses from the designs of this most expensive and elegant of modistes, she would not have been shocked, but merely puzzled as to why he would be inclined to spend his money so lavishly upon a series of passing fancies.

Fortunately Madame was far too wise and experienced an old fox to mistake Sally for one of Gervais' light-skirts. Her practiced eye instantly percieved a young relation, up from some dreary provincial town in the country, about to make her debut upon society, and placed by her parents in the capable hands of her stylish brother or cousin.

When Gervais casually informed Madame Céleste that the young lady was no debutante at all, but the new Lady Marchman, her eyebrows moved only a fraction of an inch. So, she thought, this was the American peeress of whom everyone was talking. That such a fashionable personage' as Gervais had taken her up gave her an automatic cachet that Madame Céleste would stake her business the girl would not receive otherwise. Truly, she thought, this promised to be interesting.

With the genius that had elevated her to the ranks of the most fashionable modiste in London, Madame stepped back and appraised her new client, who in turn regarded her uneasily. The freckles were impossible, of course, and thankfully the problem of her maid and hairdresser, not Madame Céleste. The reddish-blond tresses, such a pity that red hair had never come into fashion, called for very careful handling of color and shade. No purples, no reds, and thank *le bon Dieu*, no debutante pastels, so trying with that fair skin. A pleasing figure, if slightly overample in the bosom and the hips, and a good height to display the lower waists and fuller skirts that were coming across the Channel from Paris this season. Like the artist she was, Madame Céleste paced about her client, frowning with thought, murmuring to herself as her assistants scurried about taking Lady Marchman's measurements and fetching needle and thread. There was a prolonged and whispered conference with Gervais; no two heads of state could have met with more seriousness and gravity as the advantages and disadvantages of various styles, colors, dresses, and gowns were debated. Sally, for whom all of this was being done, might have been a dressmaker's dummy for all that her opinion was solicited.

The outfitting of the new Lady Marchman was evidently so delicate a project that it could only be handled by experts.

At last, with many loud exclamations in French and English, Gervais and Madame Céleste reached some sort of accord. "You will come with me, if you please," Madame Céleste commanded Lady Marchman imperiously, leading away the newest peeress to a back boudoir. Uneasily, Sally looked over her shoulder at Gervais, but he impatiently waved her onward, settling himself comfortably into a sofa for a light flirtation with the prettiest of Madame's assistants.

When Sally emerged from the pink-and-white-striped boudoir a quarter-hour later, she wore a bemused look and a becoming morning dress of the palest and whitest of celestial blues, cut high to the throat with a tiny ruffle of Belgian lace, the long, full leg-o'-mutton sleeves just beginning to be seen, and a body of cambric, sewn from bodice to hem in thousands of tiny pin tucks, with a row of shell-shaped mother-of-pearl buttons closing from the neck to the waist, and a deep stiffened hem of Belgian lace and tiny lawn flowers.

"My French," Sally announced airily, "I have

just found to be less than adequate. I knew I should have studied more thoroughly."

She made a turn for Gervais, and he studied her critically. "I think that the hem must come up an inch, and I think that some of the fullness in those sleeves ought to be taken out. Tends to make a woman look thick through the waist."

Madame nodded, and one of her assistants scribbled his directives down into a notebook. Sally was firmly propelled back to the all-female world of pink stripes and white satin, still working at her French to make herself understood.

Gervais was just discovering the address of the lovely Yvonne's rooms in Camberwell when Sally emerged again, this time in pink and white stripes. "Good God, no," Gervais called vehemently before she was halfway down the salon. Madame Céleste marched her back into the dressing room, and Gervais made an elegant expression of sympathy in French when he discovered that Yvonne's family went into exile from France rather than face the restoration of the fat Bourbon king.

Successively, Sally appeared in an aquamarine ball gown of crepe de chine, trimmed with tiny seed pearls, cut rather low in the bodice and rather high in the skirt (yes); a day dress of printed daffodil silk, cleverly trimmed in tiny knots of lavender and peach riband, and a laced bodice (perhaps); a lawn walking dress with lace points at hem and sleeve with a short spencer of sky-blue merino worn over the worked net bodice (yes); a riding habit that Sally insisted she must have of dove-gray broadcloth, cut *à la militaire* with gold frogging and epaulets, and bands of gold at hem and cuff. Gervais, who did not care for horses, was indifferent about the color, but Sally was adamant, and prevailed. They compromised on a dinner dress of crepe de chine and silk tartan, done up in forest green—since Gervais thought it looked dignified, and Sally thought it dowdy—but were in total agreement that a cloth-of-gold ball gown was hideous as well as somewhat doubtful in taste and that a peau-de-soie evening dress of a somewhat unusual shade of leaf green worked all over in the most delicate embroidery with tiny fish and birds was an absolute necessity.

There was the simple matter of a spangled shawl in marsala, and a light walking coat of turned honey-rose, trimmed with bands of primrose, and a carriage coat of a rather sensible chocolate brown with bone buttons and a very cunning shawl collar. There were day dresses in Indian printed muslin and sprigged cambric, and silk nightgowns and elaborately embroidered peignoirs, covered with sunbursts.

The question of her undergarments, he left to Sally, but he insisted to her that the sensible cotton she had been used to would be nothing compared to the fit and feel of silk. Meekly she obeyed, and emerged from her fittings two hours later slightly dazed and a little elated by her new and very sophisticated wardrobe.

"I am grown to look quite elegant," she observed thoughtfully to Gervais. "I wish that it were all ready right now, so that I could take it all home and just look at it."

"The old harpy swore up and down she'd have it all altered and ready by Wednesday," Gervais said, thinking that for what the bill would come to, and it would be staggering, that was the least Madame Céleste could do.

"I suppose we shall be late to luncheon," Sally

said when they were back in the barouche. "Hope Lady Aurelia will not be too put out with me."

"Lady Aurelia does, and always has done, exactly as she pleases," Gervais answered. "Besides, we are not finished yet, oh, no. Next we visit the shoemaker, and then the milliner, and the mantua maker. I shall leave it to some understanding female to take you to your corset maker. Even I must draw the line somewhere." Gervais pulled his beaver down over his eyes and stretched out his legs.

By teatime, Sally had ordered six new pairs of slippers; a pair of riding boots from Gervais' own bootmaker; a pair of jean half-boots for walking and riding in the park, an occupation Gervais assured her was de rigueur for every fashionable Londoner; a pair of pink satin mules to lounge about in her boudoir; a very dashing leghorn hat trimmed with silk flowers; a tartan cap (tartan, Sally soon discovered, was all the rage that year); a cottage bonnet of mauve satin, trimmed with blue ribbons, a riding cap of gray felt, trimmed with several dashing gray plumes that swept beneath her chin; an ivory lawn morning cap rimmed with tiny ruches of spiderweb lace that tied beneath her chin and proclaimed her status, however doubtful, as a married lady, which was both very plain and shockingly expensive. Having dissuaded her from a cream-colored toque ornamented with a very unhappy-looking set of artificial cherries, Gervais felt expansive enough to allow her the purchase of another chipstraw hat of slightly more style, character, and freshness than her old model, and he grudgingly admitted that she looked very fetching in what he designated as countrified styles. Solely to please his taste, she allowed him to select a rather so-

phisticated affair of stiffened cambric, ruched
and gathered about the crown and spreading out
into a very wide brim that swept low over her
left cheek, of a shade of apple green, trimmed
with a plain hat band of ivory grosgrain, and tied
beneath the chin with the same riband. "Take
my word for it, you'll look dashed fetching in it,"
he said. "Riding up in a gent's phaeton in the
park with that red hair of yours."

Privately, Sally thought that she would look a
quiz in anything so extreme, but she added it to
the rest.

At teatime, they had ices at the Piazza, and
Gervais was jolted out of his vague feeling of
ennui by his amusement at Sally's interest in all
that went on around them in that busy restaurant. The most public place she had ever dined
had been the ordinary of the Hole in the Wall
Tavern in Watertown, and the experience of eating in a restaurant was quite novel for her. "I
must seem a proper bumpkin," she laughingly
admitted to Gervais as she lapped lime ice from
her spoon with the tip of her tongue, savoring
the flavor as it went down.

"On the contrary, I think it's rather charming," he replied lazily. "It's a refreshing change
from misses who are bored and jaded by it all at
the age of eighteen."

Sally threw him a wondering glance from beneath the brim of her hat, the thought flickering
through her mind that he might be thinking of
Annabella, but she refrained from comment, having no wish to spoil the day by bringing the
beauty or Peter into the conversation.

"Tell me about the Covent Garden masks," she
suggested instead, looking at him with wide and
innocent eyes.

Gervais raised an eloquent eyebrow. "Beyond the pale without question," he said firmly. "Not the sort of place where young ladies like you should be seen."

"Have you been?"

Gervais nodded. "Many times, mostly when I was younger and slightly more foolish. And never, ever, with a lady. Save once, and then I had good cause to regret allowing myself to be cuzzled into it. No, my dear coz, Gervais does not repeat mistakes twice. Besides which, to take another man's wife to one of those orgies would be beyond anything dishonorable."

Sally could tell by his tone that the subject was closed, but her curiosity was further piqued.

"How about Astley's Ampitheater?" she asked next.

Gervais grinned, looking almost boyish. "Astley's. Good God, I haven't been to Astley's since I was at Harrow."

"I think I should like to go," Sally remarked wistfully. "They have a woman who does bareback tricks on a white stallion."

Gervais removed his watch from his pocket and looked at the face. If he had other plans for that evening—and it was likely that he did—they were blithely canceled without the least twinge of guilt. Yvonne would wait in vain. "By God, Cousin Sally, I cannot think of any good reason why we can't just amble off to Astley's right now. Aunt doesn't dine until eight, and we'll have you and the barouche there by seven, if you finish that disgustingly sweet sorbet."

Sally's face lit up. "Oh, Gervais, really?" she asked. "I mean, it wouldn't be a dead bore for someone as—as fashionable and sophisticated as you, would it?"

If she was teasing him, Gervais did not notice. Grinning like the schoolboy he once had been, he stood up and offered her his arm. "Shall we depart, Lady Marchman?" he asked.

15

In the fortnight since his wife's disappearance, Peter Marchman had slept but a few hours, in those times when his exhausted body could overcome the turbulence in his mind. In the first day, he had believed that she was only out in the hills, sulking somewhere, waiting for him to come and find her. When she had not made an appearance by the evening of the second day, he began to grow anxious to the extent that he questioned the servants and cross-examined Annabella and Mrs. Marchman again and again, hoping that their memories would turn up some clue. That, from the onset, they seemed more relieved than worried about Sally's possible fate, airily remarking that the tension in the air had cleared considerably since she had betaken herself off, did not put Peter into charity with either one of them.

Indeed, as if a veil of illusion had been lifted from his eyes, he began to perceive both mother and daughter as much of the rest of the world had perceived them for a great long time; they were both selfish, hysterical neurasthenics who would go to any lengths, no matter how crude or obvious, to make their own comfort paramount over any other consideration.

Previously, he had considered his aunt rather comical, if somewhat pathetic. Now, in his anxiety and rage, he could barely stand to hear her martyred sighs as she demanded to know if the household must really be overthrown like this because of that tiresome American chit.

"Madam," Peter said in tones of ice, "you are speaking about my wife, Lady Marchman." With those words, he strode from the room to seek to organize yet another search party, leaving Mrs. Marchman the rather unsatisfactory task of having to indulge herself in a fit of the vapors without a sympathetic audience. Ring and ring as she might, no servant answered her bell, for all, together with the neighborhood, were out searching caves and spinneys, dragging millponds and creeks, in a vain search for Sally Marchman.

It was an unfortunate characteristic of Annabella's that she could never do anything with a degree of subtlety. Noticing simply that Peter was avoiding her company, she sought him out on the second night of the fruitless search, and found him alone in his study, his dinner on a tray untouched before him, a bottle of brandy, nearly empty, in his fist as he stared, with unseeing eyes and a turbulent mind, into the dead fireplace. All else had been abandoned while he frantically directed the hunt for Sally. In forty-eight hours, not so much as a ribbon had turned up. She might have disappeared off the face of the earth, vanished without a clue, he brooded guiltily, save that in his mind he could see her, alive and laughing, happy with her love for him, his love for her. And now she was gone. He had driven her away as surely as if he had raised his own hand and killed her, killed the only person he had ever loved in his life. In his tortured mind, a thousand small sins he had committed against her each rose up and turned into monsters that devoured him with guilt and remorse. Again and again, he reenacted that last night in his mind, the bitter quarrel that had driven her away from him. He racked himself with a hundred mental guilts, the pain of losing Sally far worse than the horrors of any inquisition they could put his body through. Indeed, Peter would have suffered gladly any agony, any pain that could be inflicted, if only they would let him see her again. How could he have been so blind, so enveloped in his eternal struggle with his unwanted, infernal title, this ruined estate? Duty? Too late, he understood all too clearly that his first duty had been to his wife, to red-haired, laughing Sally. To the only woman he had ever loved with all his heart and soul . . .

"Well," Annabella said in the doorway, "aren't we pensive tonight? Why don't you have Fishguard light some candles in here? This place is positively gloomy."

Haggard and stubbled, Peter looked up at her from red-rimmed eyes. Annabella—poor, silly, vain, beautiful Annabella. What man in his right mind would ever choose this simpering little fool over a woman like Sally? Good God, how could Sally ever believe that he would ever want Annabella?

Her skirts rustled as she crossed the floor and opened a window, allowing the June breeze to drift through the close room. "So stuffy in here," she prattled artlessly while he wished she would leave. "Really, Peter, I must say that you're taking all of this far too seriously. Of course, it's unpleasant, and the neighbors will talk, but it doesn't signify, does it?"

She turned and smiled at him. Peter glared back, unmoving.

Annabella's pretty lower lip thrust itself out

in a pout. "Well, it's not *my* fault, you know," she said with a whining edge in her voice. "After all, she didn't have to wear that silly dress and the jewels, did she? Anyone who'd been born to it would have known better." She primped at her hair. "I wish that you would speak to me," she whined, and stamped a slippered foot against the rug. "It's odiously unfair! Ever since she left, no one invites us to parties, and no one comes to call unless it's to make a report of some stoopid little thing. I'm dying of boredom! I am! I am!"

Dimly, through his pain, Peter perceived a woman of some nineteen or twenty summers having a tantrum that would have shamed a small, very tired child, while out there, Sally was somewhere, alive or dead, or lying in a cave or a ditch, too weak to cry out for help . . .

"I want to get out of here. I don't want to have to hear all these bad things about Sally this and Sally that. Doesn't anybody care about me?" Annabella, working herself into hysterics, was starting to scream. It was not attractive, Peter thought, wondering why he had allowed them to subject Sally to their selfish jealousies. He should have sent them both packing off to Bath. It was not as if Theresa did not have a perfectly ample income of her own . . .

"Annabella," Peter heard himself saying in a tight, controlled voice that seemed to come from somewhere else, "if you do not stop it right now, I swear before God that I will box your ears."

Perhaps the dead, calm tone of his voice convinced her that he meant what he said, for she arrested herself in midscream, her eyes large and her mouth open, staring at him in dull surprise.

"H-how could you talk that way to me?" she

demanded when she could speak again. "H-how could y-you? You love me! You don't love her! You don't! You don't!"

Some thin thread that had been holding Peter together through the past forty-eight hours began to unravel. With awful deliberation, he rose from the desk, and she took a step backward, clutching her breast in dramatic horror such as she had seen actresses do on the stage. But behind it, there was a fear that was real enough at last. He could sense it.

"Know this," Lord Marchman said with infinite fatigue, "just know this, Annabella. I would see you burning in hell if it would bring Sally back for just one minute of time."

Annabella's mouth opened and closed soundlessly before she emitted a strangled shriek and fled to spread the word that Peter was going mad.

Most believed that he was finally coming to his senses. Some prayed that it was not too late.

Their prayers were answered almost a week later. After the initial excitement, the enthusiasm for the hunt had gradually begun to fade, and men went back to their jobs, sad, but satisfied with the knowledge that there was no area of the countryside, no local or passing stranger who had been left unquestioned or unsearched. The magistrate, pessimistic but sympathetic with Peter's burden, had printed up handbills, and had sent inquiries and particulars to Bow Street. But nothing had turned up Sally, only vague and fleeting rumors that she had been seen at a gypsy horse fair in Birmingham, or spotted in a carriage in Anglesey.

In his grief, Peter abandoned all pretense of working at the unchanging knot of estate problems. He spent day after day closeted in his office, seeing no one save Fishguard, who brought him his untouched food and his bottles of brandy.

This day, Fishguard also brought in the post. "I think sir, that I espied Lady Aurelia's handwriting among the letters," Fishguard said as he laid the stack of missives on the desk. "She might have some news, sir."

Peter nodded, waiting until the butler had left the room before he eagerly tore into the letter bearing Lady Aurelia's old-fashioned, spidery fist. She did, indeed, have news.

Eagerly, and with the first glimmer of hope he had felt in many days, Peter scanned the crossed and recrossed epistle.

"Think it my duty to tell you that Sarah is residing in London with me . . ." he read aloud. "Since her arrival here, she has been quite busy . . . happily occupied with the pleasures of fashionable society. A success . . . much in demand . . . Almack's . . . driving in the park with Gervais . . ." Peter frowned. "Gervais and I have managed to bring her quite into fashion . . . much more of a credit to me than Annabella's Season . . . Seems quite attached to Gervais and he to her . . . everywhere together . . . can be no breath of scandal, of course, since they are cousins by marriage. . . . She will agree to a divorce so that you will be free to marry Annabella . . . intends to procure same in America, much simpler over there, no scandal dragged through House of Lords . . . has not said, but am confident she will marry Gervais . . . doubtless all for the best . . ."

Peter crushed the letter in his fist, frowning. Sally divorce him and marry Gervais? Not bloody likely, while he was still breathing! Now that he knew that she was alive and well and safe with that meddling old tyrant, Aunt Aurelia, Peter felt more alive than he had in a fortnight. As long as Sally was alive, there was hope.

He leapt to his feet and flung open the door. "Fishguard!" he bellowed. "Food, hot water, and pack my bags. Send for the phaeton! I'm leaving for London at once," he shouted, so loud that the entire household could hear.

Oblivious to his unwashed and unshaven state, Peter strode down the corridor toward the morning room. As he had suspected, he found both Aunt Theresa and Annabella, hot in perusal of the *Court Circular.*

When they saw him enter, both women gasped with fright, and he suddenly realized, not without amusement, that he must look like a madman. Which he supposed he was.

"Aunt," he announced quite calmly, "I am going to London to fetch my wife back to her own home. Do you comprehend? *Her own home.* Marchman Place. I suspect that I shall not be gone above a week, but when I return, I expect that you will have removed yourself to the Dower House, or if you wish, I shall put my man of business instantly in the way of procuring a comfortable house for you in Bath. Since you have frequently expressed a wish to retire to your own establishment in Laura Place, I see no reason to place any obstacle in your way. Your jointure is quite ample, and with what you have managed to save over the years living at Marchman Place, I am quite certain that you will allow yourself every comfort—including the endless quacking of humbug doctors to whom you seem to be addicted."

He grinned rather diabolically and was about to close the door upon one of what he was certain would be Mrs. Marchman's more violent fits of hysterics, when he had a second thought. "And, you will also be good enough to remove your daughter with you, if you please."

The shrieks made a delightful sound as they echoed down the stone corridors. Aunt Theresa was always prone to hysterics when faced with the prospect of parting with her own money.

It was the work of an hour to be ready to depart for London. His phaeton and team were waiting for him in the stableyard, and Peter swung easily up into the perch, running the thin reins between his fingers before he noted a cloaked figure huddled in the corner beneath the bonnet.

"Damn, Annabella," he exclaimed impatiently, "can't you get it through your head that I don't want to deal with you?"

"Take me to London, and you shall never have to deal with me again," Annabella announced in tones of high tragedy. "I would rather die than live in Laura Place. Bath!" she shuddered. "Nothing but dowdies and dowagers and Assemblies that end at ten."

"At this point, I can picture no fate you deserve more," Peter said dryly. "Now, will you get down, or shall I throw you onto the cobbles?"

"You don't understand," Annabella whined, wringing her hands. "I read your letter from Aunt Aurelia! It was only then that I realized that I don't want to marry you—I want to marry Gervais!"

"Good God," Peter remarked. Knowing Annabella, he suspected that it was precisely the sort of capricious idea she would take into her scatterbrained head. He began to laugh.

"Well, I don't think it's one bit amusing," Annabella said stiffly. "I've been in love with him all along, and I've been blinded by your title."

"Gervais may have it, for all of me! God, I wish I could give it to him." Peter laughed. "The awful thing is, Gervais is such a fool that he's been in love with you anytime these past few years. Good God, he'll probably have you, too."

"I was quite a success in London. I had several offers for my hand," Annabella exclaimed indignantly. "After all, I am a beauty!"

"And a scatterbrained ninny to boot. Oh, my stars and garters, let Gervais have you. I daresay if anyone would have the patience to pound some sort of human feeling into that tiny brain of yours, it would be him."

"Yes, and I will be in the first stare of fashion, also," Annabella said complacently.

"Yes, I suppose you will." Peter's tone was thoughtful. "Well, a match made, well, made somewhere, at any rate."

Annabella flounced. "Quick, let's be off before Mama starts looking for me. Bath, indeed! That was not very kind of you, Peter."

"Neither was your mother's treatment of my wife. No more arguing, now. We're off to London, and if we can untangle this knot, Annabella, then I will say that you and I have done mighty well by this day's work."

He whipped up the team and they sprang to.

"Marry Gervais!" Peter laughed as they moved out of the stableyard. "Marry Gervais! I do believe that you might actually care for that fop. Marry Gervais, indeed!"

16

Unlike such leisured travelers as Lady Aurelia, Lord Marchman pulled into the yard of the Four Swans, calling not for a bed and a warm nuncheon, but for a change of horses, and quick at that.

As the ostlers sprung to obey, Annabella was left to make her own way down from the high perch, continuing the litany of complaints she had poured into Peter's ears since they had left Marchman Place. He drove much too fast over the rutted roads and had almost overturned them passing the Bristol Mail with inches to spare. He cared naught for her comfort nor safety, having provided her with not so much as a lap robe against the mud and dust of the road with the consequence that her lovely traveling pelisse and orange jean boots were quite ruined, her hair was a fright, and her feathered bonnet an utter quiz. Upon finding, from one monosyllabic grunt from Peter, that they would not dine, the beauty began to wail, wringing her hands and stamping her feet in the beginnings of a first-class tantrum that was attracting the interest of several persons.

"I won't! I won't!" she screeched, working herself into a frenzy of hysteria.

Peter, the past six weeks since his return increasingly less charmed with Annabella's petulant personality, wondered what he had ever seen adorable and charming in her. Perhaps what made these qualities interesting in a child of sixteen were no longer becoming in a woman nearly twenty.

After nearly five hours of her unmitigated complaining, he would gladly have hired a post chaise to convey her back to Marchman Place, save that he knew that any such suggestion would lead to outbursts far worse.

Fortunately, he was saved from delivering a very strong set-down by the innkeeper's wife, who had known Annabella since she was a child, and now bustled forth from the kitchen, wiping her hands on her apron and clucking in a maternal fashion.

"Here, now, Mr. Peter," she said, leading the sobbing Annabella away, "she never did travel well, poor lamb. What she needs is a hot posset and a bit of a nuncheon."

"I could not put a morsel between my lips," Annabella declared firmly, but allowed herself to be led away by Mrs. Nudgy and her satellites.

Peter, cursing the delay, sat down upon the mounting block and placed his dark head between his hands. But when Mrs. Nudgy bustled out with a pint of ale and a bit of bread and cheese, he did not refuse them for himself, and found himself the better for it.

The mud and dust wiped away from her face, her hair combed and her pelisse brushed, Annabella resumed the trip in a slightly better frame of mind, only once admonishing Peter to mind a sharp turn in the road, and pettishly complaining that all the garments she had stuffed into her bandbox would be sadly ruined.

Since Peter encouraged neither subject for con-

versation, but only drove toward the metropolis
as if the very devil himself were after him,
Annabella, with a long-suffering sigh, contented
herself with calling him the greatest beast in
nature, that no power on earth could ever per-
suade her to wish to marry him, if he were the
possessor of a dukedom. "Sally may have you, for
all I care! You are not only grown odious and
uncivil, but quite, quite mad," she declared, removing a mirror from her reticule to examine
her hair in the fading light.

Thus was the happy journey passed to London. When they reached Finchley Common, Peter thought he had never been so glad to see the
metropolis in his entire life, unable to decide if
ridding himself of Annabella's company or re-
gaining that of his wife were more important to
him.

Nothing could have been more vast than the
sigh of relief he gave as he pulled up his phaeton
and sweating team before the compact mansion
on Upper Mount Street. Evidently, Annabella
was of the same feeling, for as he handed her
down from the trap, she said pettishly, "I have
not the least desire to ride with you ever again,
Peter. Compared to Gervais, you are the merest
whipster."

Peter's response to this was fortunately lost in
the hammering of the big brass knocker that was
almost instantly, as if he had been waiting for it,
answered by the looming presence of Duddle
himself.

This individual looked down at the pair of
bedraggled figures before him and opened one
eye. "Well, now, my lady said you would be here,
and my lady is always right, bless me stars!"

"Where is my wife?" Peter demanded, in no

mood to tolerate the usual arch familiarities of Duddle.

The man looked distinctly hurt. He rubbed his jaw. "Well, now, I couldn't say, not being her keeper. She could be at Lady Sefton's rout party, or she could be at the opera, or she could be havin' a look-in at Almack's—"

"Almack's," Annabella exclaimed, much shocked. "Whoever would give *her* vouchers to Almack's pray tell me?"

"Princess Lieven *and* Mrs. Drummond Burrell," Duddle replied grandly. "And she didn't have to beg for them from Sally Jersey like *some* misses we all know," he added.

This barb struck home, for Annabella flushed. "Well!" she said. "Are we to stand on the steps all night, or do you intend to let us in?"

Duddle inclined his head to one side. "Well, I suppose I can let you in, Miss Annabella, seein's how I ain't had no word from her ladyship to the contrary. But I've got strict orders to refuse admittance to Mr. Peter—Lord Marchman, if I may so say."

Peter clenched his jaw. "See here, Duddle, what d'you mean, you've got strict orders not to let me in?"

"Just as I said, sir. Lady Aurelia said you were not to be admitted. She doesn't want you upsettin' Lady Marchman, right in the middle of her Season. Quite grand, you know, we've become," he added with satisfaction. "Indeed, you might say that're all the crack. Hostesses vyin' wid one another to get us to their parties, ball in her ladyship's honor at Devonshire House, tea parties and rout parties and I don't know what all."

"You're just saying that because you dislike me so much and like her," Annabella pouted.

Duddle shook his head. " 'Taint so," he announced adamantly. "I don't have no say in who's fashionable and who's not. My lady and Mr. Gervais, now, they were the ones who contrived it all. Why, you wouldn't know Lady Marchman, not now! As fine as a fivepence, she is. Mr. Gervais went out to that Madame Céleste's and had her turned out as fine as a fashionplate. Wouldn't know her comin' and goin', and busy, busy all the day long she is—in the morning, there's a parade of gentlemen callin', bearin' poetry an' nosegays—"

"Gentlemen calling?" Lord Marchman demanded in an awful voice, shades of his courtship rising before his eyes.

Duddle nodded with satisfaction. "Lots of gentlemen, an' all proper top-o'-the-trees they are, too, no o' your swells and fortune-hunters. Why, there's Alvaney, and Sir Clifton Hough, and Mr. Tifton-White—"

"Tifton-White? I'll have it out with him! We were at Harrow together," Lord Marchman exclaimed, knotting his fists.

"Tiffy!" Annabella wailed, for he had been one of her most devoted suitors.

The butler repressed a smile of satisfaction. "Of course, Mr. Gervais practically lives in my lady's pocket, so to speak—" he hinted, clearly enjoying himself.

Annabella wailed.

"Oh, be quiet, do, you silly goose! I need to think," Peter snarled in a manner that quite made Duddle's brows sail into his wig. He was beginning to sense the layout of the land.

"An' the flowers!" the butler continued, rolling his eyes. "Like a regular hothouse it is in there, smellin' of April and May."

"April and May," Peter repeated heavily.

"More nor when Miss Annabella were here for her Season," Duddle said complacently. "And the ladies who come to call and send their cards about! There's Lady Jersey, and Lady Sefton, and Lady Ombersely, and Mrs. Drummond Burrell and Princess Lieven—and a whole score besides, all wantin' Miss Sally to ride up in the park with them, or attend the opera or the theater or the concerts. Right fond of concerts, Miss Sally is, and to see her watchin' Kean at the theater, you'd think she'd died and gone to heaven."

"Bluestocking," Annabella sniffed.

"Duddle! Duddle! Whatever is that unearthly fracas?" demanded an imperious voice from the stairs. "I must have my sleep if Miss Sally is to have her ball tomorrow."

"Now you've gone and done it," Duddle said wisely as Lady Aurelia, attended by Hurlock and wrapped in a voluminous old-fashioned dressing gown of rose damask, a white lawn cap tied securely beneath her chin, and a pair of carpet slippers slapping at her heels, majestically descended the stairs, her malacca cane tapping at each step, Hurlock right behind, her attire quite similar, her demeanor every iota as haughty, determined to defend her mistress to the death.

Pausing on the landing, Lady Aurelia surveyed her relations with a basilisk stare. "And what," she inquired in arctic tones, "does *this* mean?"

"It means, my lady," Duddle said, "that Mr. Peter—Lord Marchman and Miss Annabella have arrived, lookin', presumably, for Lady Marchman."

"And Gervais," Annabella put in a quavering voice, "if you please."

If the tips of the dowager's thin lips quivered, no one could notice. "Lady Marchman, as I am certain Duddle has informed you, Peter, is out for the evening, and I do not know when I expect her to come in. She wore a ball dress, so I would expect to see her not until three or later. In the morning, I shall expect her to sleep in, since tomorrow evening I am giving a ball in her honor. To which I recall sending neither of you invitations," she added firmly.

Annabella, always terrified of Lady Aurelia, whimpered.

Peter was, however, made of sterner stuff, and eyed his aunt with a fortitude she admired, even if she kept such admiration well hidden beneath a mask of hauteur.

"Aunt, I have come to claim my wife," Peter declared firmly. "There has been a terrible misunderstanding. Perhaps I have not been all that I would be as a husband, but now I have seen my mistakes. My only wish is to make Sally as happy as I can, to make her mistress of Marchman Place. Aunt Theresa is removing to Bath, and if Gervais truly wants to marry this scatterbrained nitwit, he is more than welcome to her for all of me! Although I cannot for the life of me see how anyone, even that man-milliner Gervais, would want so vain, selfish, spoiled, hoydenish a creature as my cousin."

"Slowtop! You farmer, always reeking of the stables and the fields, falling asleep after dinner and never wanting to do anything the least amusing—and to ride into London with you like a farmwife! It is more than one can stand!"

"As you will, madam." Peter bowed. He looked at his aunt with a cool Marchman fierceness that matched her own. "Aunt Aurelia, perhaps I have been careless, but after a man has scoured the countryside, expecting only God knows what in every nook and spinney—only to find her merrily dancing away the London nights, he has a right to at least be granted an audience with her."

"Then you may be here tomorrow evening at eight, Peter. I trust you forgot a suitable set of evening clothes, if you own one? I thought as much. Perhaps Gervais may suit as well, since you are both of a size. I think that you may also stay at Gervais' in the Albany this night, as I do not wish to have Sally upset by your sudden appearance. As for you, Annabella, I see no recourse but to allow you to stay here, although you are a very tiresome girl and liable to upset the household! Given you a ride, has he, in that rackety phaeton of his? You look like something the cat dragged in. Come on, then, Hurlock will put you to bed. I am very tired and fagged to death of quarreling, so we will say no more this evening."

With an imperious gesture, she summoned Annabella up the stairs, leaving Peter to stare openmouthed after his great-aunt.

"Just between you and me, sir," Duddle said confidentially, for Peter had always been a favorite of his, "Mr. Gervais called for Miss Sally at nine—and she was carrying a pink domino under one arm."

"Vauxhall Gardens!" Peter exclaimed. "That coxcomb would take her to Vauxhall, of all places in London! Good God, I shall call him out!"

"Lower your voice, sir, iffen you please," Duddle begged with an anxious glance at the stairway. "Iffen Lady Aurelia were to hear as much of breath of it, she'd have Miss Sally's head for breakfast, and yours and Mr. Gervais' for lunch!"

"And yours for dinner, I'll wager, Duddle. Where is your fine Italian hand in all of this?" Peter asked grimly.

"Well, sir, she only said that she had a craving to see the sights, and I mentioned Vauxhall, not thinkin' that she was like a babe unborn, so to speak, and not really up to every rig and row in town—"

"Vauxhall! Good God, Duddle, have you lost your noodle? Every sort of fast, depraved, go-mad thing happens there, and in the worst possible company!"

"As well you might know, sir, since you was mighty fine fond of the place in your Oxford days—"

"That was my Oxford days, and very soon I outgrew the notion. Aunt Aurelia is quite correct in forbidding Sally such a place. Gervais must be quite mad."

"Well, sir, my lady—Miss Sally had her face set upon seein' the place, and neither Mr. Gervais nor I could dissuade her from the idea. You know what she's like when she's taken a notion to her noodle. Lady Aurelia thinks she's attending a concert of ancient music."

"Ancient music!" Peter spit out.

Duddle nodded so vehemently that his wig slipped askew.

"Precisely so, but with Mr. Gervais to look after her, nought could happen to her at Vauxhall, sir. Wraps her in cotton wool, he does."

"I'll wager he does," Peter exclaimed, snapping his whip against his boot in a way that bode no good for the elegant Gervais.

"Exactly so, sir," Duddle said faintly, watching with unconcealed fascination as Peter bounded down the steps two at a time and made a graceful leap into his phaeton, heading, Duddle was certain, for Vauxhall Gardens.

He was, however, wrong on that score, for it was not fifteen minutes later that Peter's phaeton pulled up before Gervais' elegant apartments at the Albany.

Here he was pleased to rouse up Yelping, his cousin's very elegant and very expensive gentleman's gentleman, a haughty individual who had always viewed Peter's somewhat careless sartorial displays with professional dismay. This evening, the sight of Peter's mud splattered driving coat, his crushed neckcloth, and the wild disarray of his dark locks was almost enough to give Yelping a fit of deep glooms. But before he could contemplate, with a shudder, the mangled and tarnished conditions of Lord Marchman's driving boots, that gentleman had gripped him fiercely by the silken lapels of his very fine dressing gown and was glaring at him in such a devilish way that he was reminded of the old lord himself.

"Yelping, if you do not tell me at once where your master has gone for the evening, I shall have your liver and your lights. And don't say a concert of ancient music, because I know he's at Vauxhall Gardens with Lady Marchman."

Yelping managed to swallow hard once or twice. Clearly, the new Lord Marchman had succumbed to the unfortunate madnesses of the old lord. He could only nod his head, being unable to breathe.

"Good," Peter breathed, his features determined. "Now, I know that your master has more than one domino in his wardrobe. Fetch it to me at once."

Yelping did as he was bid, and in a moment Peter was in possession of a black silk mask that hung to his shoulders. "I shall be sleeping on your master's couch tonight. Leave a light on for me," he commanded on his way out the door. "Oh, and have a man see to m' horses!"

"Yes, sir," Yelping said faintly, dabbing his brow with a handkerchief.

In a very short time, Peter's hackney carriage drew up before the stone archway that admitted all the world to Vauxhall. Seventy-five years ago the pleasure gardens might have been as respectable and sedate as the Sydney Gardens of Bath, where one might, with perfect propriety, wander among the botanical interests, watch the fountain displays, and ooh and aah at the fireworks displays while nibbling at an ice or sipping punch. But in their decline during the Regency, Vauxhall had become notorious as a place where every sort of humanity—from pickpockets and Covent Garden abbesses—convened to rub shoulders with the very highest bucks of the ton and most daring ladies of society. Beneath the requisite masks, every sort of liaison and assignation was not only countenanced, but actually encouraged, for the grounds were filled with secluded grottoes and man-made caves just right for trysting, and the daring music played by the band of the very bawdiest tunes then in fashion. The types of familiarities that would never be taken in respectable restaurants such as the Piazza were regularly expected and practiced here, heavily oiled by the overpriced and constantly flowing champagne punches served by waiters as lewd as their customers.

The music was blaring into his ears even as Lord Marchman paid his admission of one and six, shrugging impatiently at the blandishments of a woman in a low-cut gown and a bright feathered mask as he elbowed his way, none too gently, through the crowd of revelers, looking for Sally's pink domino.

Dominoes there were a plenty, he noticed, with gritted teeth, but none that would be called pink, although every other shade of the rainbow was in evidence, and someone in a scarlet mask trimmed with pearls was most persistent in attempting to gain his attentions in the most vulgar language he had heard off a troop ship.

He scanned up and down the public banquettes, where fat chits and their families gazed down upon the proceedings with the utmost amusement as waiters served huge joints of beef and the ever-flowing champagne punch.

Over his head fireworks exploded loudly, in contrast to the wheezing music of the band, making it hard for him to identify a single individual in the thick crowd.

Slowly and terribly, it began to sink into his head that Gervais and Sally might be in one of the grottoes in the back of this inferno, and he purposely made his way through the crowd, putting aside a large matron in pink and white stripes to attain this goal, when he thought that he caught sight of a rose-colored domino over a white gown that looked somehow familiar, heading in the same direction before she was obscured by that same drunken and indignant matron who seemed determined to read him a lecture as incomprehensible as it was vile.

When at last he was able to break away from her, Marchman called for Sally, thrusting his head into a great many secluded and occupied cul-de-sacs where his presence was roundly reviled by the occupants, none of whom was Gervais or Sally.

Feeling very much as if a pair of horns were

placed upon his head, Peter, unembarrassed, continued onward, blundering from yet one more compromising situation into another, without so much as mumbling his apologies, until at last, down a quiet, fern-lined path, he parted the curtains to see the unmistakable shine upon his cousin's Hessians raised high above the petticoats of a female upon a couch.

"Gervais!" Peter bellowed, his Marchman temper out of control now. "Up, man, and name your weapons!"

There was a rustle and a series of increasingly hysterical imperatives in French, and Peter blinked in to the dim light to see that the female Gervais (for those were his Hessians—who else would have such a shine?) was entertaining was definitely *not* Sally, and quite upset about it, too.

"I say, cousin," Gervais said irritably, looking up from Yvonne's luscious form without the least surprise. "Never thought I would see *you* in town. And here of all places. Perhaps Yvonne has a friend for you—"

"Coxcomb!" Peter exclaimed, finally beginning to feel faintly embarrassed. "Where is my wife?"

Lazily buttoning up his shirt, Gervais raised an eyebrow. "Don't be a Roman husband, Peter. Don't become you. Sally's worth more than that. Certainly wouldn't bring her to a place like that, you know. Made that mistake once, lived to regret it."

"She's here, all right," Peter said, breathing heavily. "I just saw her pink domino and a sort of yellow flowered striped dress."

Gervais yawned. "Your wife, my dear cousin, is at this very moment drowsing her way through an evening of ancient music at Lady Bower's. Left her there myself, and mad as fire she was about it too, but you know as well as I do that this is no place for an innocent like Cousin Sally." He patted Yvonne's hip. "Come, be a good little French girl and get dressed. My neckcloth is quite, quite ruined." He buttoned his pants nonchalantly. "I say, don't you think that a butter and bottle striped waistcoat is all that is good for Vauxhall?" he asked idly.

"Well, how could she be at Lady Bower's when I just saw her glittering through the crowd in a rose satin domino and that evening dress of hers, the one with the sprigged stripes and the whatya-maycallit hem all done up in those dashed stripes?" Peter demanded.

Gervais' long fingers paused upon the infinitesimal buttons of his waistcoat, and a sudden strong look passed over his careless expression. "Hang you for the inobservant fool that you are, Peter! That's no gown of Sally's but of Annabella's! What in blazes would she be doing here?"

"She came down here with me, in search of you," Peter said. "And you may have her, if only you'll get her off my hands. More selfish rattle-brained, idiotic female I never met in my life."

"Have her? Good God, I mean to marry her! How like her to come here, of all places. But there's no time to explain right now. I must of course rescue her again from the consequences of folly before some loose fish attempts to carry her off again as he did last time." He wound his neckcloth about his stock. "I can see that I shall have my hands full enough of her fits and starts to make it every bit a marriage *à la mode*. But what can I say? With her faults intact, she is still a beauty, and still the great love of my life."

"But you and Sally—"

"Cousin Sally is like the very best of sisters to

one, old man. It is plain to everyone but you that it's you she wants, although I am no more able to figure out why to that than to my own profound attachment to dear Annabella. Well''—He shrugged himself into his jacket. If there had been a mirror, he would have primped, Peter thought, watching him break off a sprig of jasmine and thrust it into his buttonhole. Satisfied that he was complete to a turn for his role of rescuing maidens, he handed the stunned yet smiling Yvonne several folded notes, made his bow, and escaped.

"Now," he said, completely businesslike, and a stunned Peter could only trail along in his wake as he picked his way through the crowds, as if he knew precisely where he was going.

And indeed, it seemed that he did, for in a secluded alcove beneath a statue of Venus, it seemed that the lady in the pink domino was being threatened by a very large, villainous person in what appeared to be a black tablecloth cut with eyes for a domino.

Gervais rather looked as if he wished he were carrying a sword, rather than his trim ebony walking stick, and Peter, whose recent experiences with Annabella rather inclined him toward letting her chips fall where they could, was still gentleman enough to gauge his fists against such a bruiser.

"I say here, my good man," Gervais drawled, tapping that individual on the shoulder with his stick.

"Oooooh!" came a familiar wail, and Annabella pulled back the pink domino to reveal her lovely face, gazing at Gervais as if he were Saint George.

"Here, sir, is yer prize, an' glad enough I am to let you claim 'er," growled Duddle. "When I seed her tripping outta the house with that domino that Hurlock brought back and laid out on Miss Sally's bed, I knew she was up to no good, just like before."

"Well, I can believe it! Annabella, damn, will I never cure you of this fatal attraction you have for Vauxhall Gardens? You will recall the last time you insisted I bring you here, you were so offended by the place that you refused my suit upon the spot."

"I was wrong, Gervais! I know that now," she cried, allowing him to wrap her into his arms just strongly enough for passion, but not so strongly as to crumple his necktie. "Oh, please, take me home. I overheard Duddle on the stairs, telling Peter that you had brought Sally here, and I determined that I would prevent you from making a serious mistake. I had to see you!"

"Couldn't it have waited?" Gervais asked reasonably.

"Had to follow her along to be sure no harm came to her," Duddle said. "Knowin' what she's like."

"Well, my good man, you won't have to look after her any longer, promise you that," Gervais drawled, his beloved in the crook of his arm. "Takin' her off to Gretna Green this very moment."

"Not in that horrid phaeton," Annabella exclaimed, somewhat unromantically.

"Nonsense. Wake up Madame Céleste right now and have you outfitted up right. Take along a maid for you, one of her women, taking little thing named Yvonne. Always thought a French maid added a touch of style," Gervais added without so much as batting an eyelid at Peter, who could not suppress his grin.

"Well, I'm glad that's settled," Duddle said with a loud sigh.

"But I still want to see my wife," Peter insisted.

Duddle rubbed his chin, looking at Peter thoughtfully. "Well, sir, my orders are not to let you into the house. But then, you know the Lord helps as helps themselves. Better we ought to mosey on toward home. A rare night it's been."

17

Perhaps never in its august history had Upper Mount Street seen the moonlight sight of two men, one of medium height in a stained driving coat, the other a mountain in what appeared to be a black tablecloth, staring up at the front wall of Lady Aurelia Marchman's highly respectable mansion, gazing upon the thick trellises of wisteria that climbed along the solid brick.

"Are you sure it will hold?" Peter was saying doubtfully, grasping a tendril as thick as a man's thigh as if he expected it to part from the wall in his hand.

"Hold it will an' all, sir," Duddle reassured him. "That there vine's been a growing up that there wall sinct Queen Anne's time. All you need to do is get a grip, and well, it's a matter of hand-over-handing it, if you get my lay."

"Did you try the casement lay before you entered the ring?" Peter asked, not quite sarcastically.

Duddle smiled mysteriously. "Oh, I've tried my hand at many things, Mr. Peter. But not being much in the petticoat line, the casement lay has never been one of my frobbles, so speak."

Looking at Duddle's considerable bulk, Lord Marchman could believe this, and might have said so had not Duddle suddenly hissed, pointing upward toward the windows of the rose chamber.

"It would seem my lady is retiring for the night," he observed.

"No better time for a husband to interview his own wife," Peter observed between his teeth. "But to think that the day would come when I should have to do this—"

"Best do it before the watch makes his rounds," Duddle observed anxiously. "Else we both liable to end up in the box."

Peter needed no further encouragement, and cursing the smooth soles of his driving boots, he began to mount the heavy vine. It was rougher work than he had expected it to be. The old bark was slippery, causing him to lose his toehold from time to time, but as he scaled past the second story, he thought he heard Duddle, somewhat oiled by Vauxhall Gardens champagne punch, encouraging him from below with such phrases as he thought suitable and sporting; and gritting his teeth, Peter clung on desperately, inching himself through the scratchy greenery until he reached the window he thought was his wife's bedchamber.

His heart was rewarded for his labors, when as he shifted his weight from the vine to a precarious position of half-clinging to the sill, he actually caught sight of Sally herself, seated at her dressing table in a sumptuous peignoir of India figured silk, reading what appeared to be a book by candlelight.

Oblivious to her observer, Sally yawned, idly pulling the ivory pins from her strawberry hair.

Peter had to admit to himself that she looked very good. Evidently London life had agreed with her, for she had dropped some weight, and there was a becoming flush in her cheeks. In fact, to his yearning eyes, she seemed to be blooming, long lashes dropped over her cheeks, her forehead serene in the light of a candle burning on the nightstand.

Leaning precariously forward, Peter rapped his knuckles against the glass pane.

Sally started, looking about the room, clutching her book to her chest. Protectively, she placed a hand against her abdomen, reaching for the bell pull.

"Sally!" Peter hissed.

Her eyes grew very round and she stared directly at him, her mouth falling open in surprise. Peter, mildly annoyed that a woman should be in the least surprised by the unexpected appearance of her estranged husband at her second-story window, apparently suspended in midair, well past the witching hour, grimaced, trying to open the sash a little further and still maintain his balance. "Sally, let me in," he exclaimed in tones muffled by a mouthful of wisteria vine.

Sally merely continued to stare, utterly and awfully fascinated. Perhaps this was fortunate, for at that moment Hurlock entered the room unbidden, *tsking* as she did so.

"Reading in bed by candlelight at all hours, my lady!" That gaunt female clucked with the air of a retainer long in Sally's service. "Here now, that will never do, not in your condition. And that injurious night air. So unhealthy, my lady," she added, trodding purposely toward the casement.

Peter, his fingers hooked beneath the window, saw himself a dead man, but at that moment, Sally said quickly, "Oh, pray, Hurlock, leave it open. These summer nights are so stuffy that some nights I can barely breathe. And you know what the doctor said about fresh air."

Hurlock paused in the middle of the rug, then turned as Peter heaved a sigh of relief. "Just as you like, my lady! If Doctor says fresh air, then fresh air it shall be, although we consider night air miasmic, provoking to aches and chills."

Sally giggled quite credibly. "You sound quite like Mrs. Marchman, Hurlock," she said with a mock yawn as the abigail fluffed up her pillows, removed the book from her hands, and extinguished the candle.

"Be that as it may, Miss Sally," Hurlock rejoined tartly. "I was brought up in service to never criticize my betters, but if we're to talk of that *one*—well, what a night, what a night, with that Miss Annabella appearing and disappearing as if she were made of mist, and then Duddle out after her and a certain someone making a most unexpected appearance. What a night, indeed! Well, Miss Sally, my lamb, you put your head upon that pillow and close your eyes, for I daresay Lady Aurelia's so wrought up that not a wink of sleep shall either of us have this night. Doubtless I shall have to read my way through Gibbon before she closes her eyes." With these words, Miss Hurlock was out the door, closing it firmly behind herself, her muttering trailing down the hallway.

Sally counted to ten before she was out of bed, easing the heavy casement upward and propping her face in her hands upon the sill to stare at Peter with an unreadable expression.

"By rights, I suppose I ought to call to that watchman I see down there deep in conversation with Duddle and his leather flask," she said in her matter-of-fact voice, as if appearing husbands were an everyday occurrence. She hoped he could not hear the thunder of her heart as she gazed upon his face. "Or perhaps I ought to simply slam the window on your fingers, Peter Marchman!"

A sharp retort rose to his lips, but the sight of her face, pale in the gaslight, with that splash of freckles across her nose, silenced all anger. "Sally, if you only knew what you've done to me. I thought you dead," he whispered, wanting to take her hand and unable to do so, lest he lose his precarious balance. "You don't know—we searched everywhere—every spinney, every crag, every cave and millpond—"

Her expression softened slightly. "I suppose it was very bad of me not to leave you a note. Usually I am so good at that sort of thing. Remembering to leave notes, not their contents! But I was beyond bearing all things by then—I only saw my own temper. And yours, of course. If Aunt Aurelia had not happened by, I should be on my way home to Maryland—"

"You could have written me one line—"

"I needed time to think, Peter, I was used shockingly badly by Annabella and your aunt." She put a fist to her mouth. "Oh, and I swore to myself I should say nothing. Incidentally, might one ask precisely where the lovely Annabella has gone, since you had the temerity to bring her here, of all places?"

If there was a spark of jealousy behind her eyes, Peter was too amused to notice it. "You will never believe, Sally! She insisted that I bring her down to London so that she could marry Gervais. She thought that you and he were at Vauxhall Gardens—"

"And stole the domino I was planning to wear—

save that Gervais said under no circumstances would he ever take me there, and was in fact meeting a milliner's 'prentice named Yvonne, so I would not fit into his plans at all. I ended up at a concert of ancient music, after all, and very dull it was!"

"Well, Sally my love, the long and the short of it is that Gervais, Annabella, and this Yvonne person are all on their way to Gretna Green, and if they should fall into the pits of hell en route, I for one should not mourn. A more henwitted, tiresome, selfish, scatterbrained female than my cousin I have never seen in my life."

"Annabella—Yvonne, Gervais—Gretna Green," Sally exclaimed, pealing with laughter. But Peter's description of his cousin had not eluded her either. "But Annabella cannot—that is, Yvonne—not even Gervais would—"

"Along as the French maid," Peter said grimly. "Gervais insisted upon awakening Madame Céleste in order to trousseau his intended for a Scots honeymoon."

Sally laughed, and Peter realized how much he had missed that merry peal. "Now I shall never go to Vauxhall," she said with mock sadness. "And of course, I am very fashionable, you know, so I go everywhere. Lady Aurelia has seen to that. I was presented at court, Peter."

"Yes, I daresay you were, my love, and I wish I had seen you in hoops and feathers. Doubtless I would have had to grow hysterical."

Sally narrowed her eyes. "Well, my Lord Marchman," she said slowly, in cool tones, "you may think me provincial and American, but I will have you know that London society has declared me a success. I am invited everywhere, including places Annabella and Mrs. Marchman could never have dreamed of visiting."

"The Vauxhall?" Peter retorted, stung in spite of himself.

"Should you like to see my Almack's vouchers?" Sally hissed.

"No, I should only like to see you home and at my sid—" Peter started to say when the room behind them was flooded by a brace of candles.

Looking rather like a very comical pair of Macbeth's witches, Lady Aurelia, her hair in braids and her robe flowing about her ample figure, led Miss Hurlock into the room.

"What's this? What's this?" Lady Aurelia demanded. "Peter, you were always the most plaguey sort of a boy. I will not have you disturbing the dear gel! Off with you at once, and tell Duddle I said to be certain that you sleep tonight at Gervais'! We shall see you tomorrow at eight precisely before Sarah's ball! And mind that you wear Gervais' formal clothes and not those rags of your own."

Miss Hurlock nodded firmly, evidently ready to follow Lady Aurelia's directives with a whack of the candlestick if necessary.

There was nothing for it; exchanging a speaking look with Sally, a chastened Peter began his slow and precarious descent of the wisteria vine.

18

When the next evening, precisely at eight, Peter, slightly constricted by Gervais' impeccable, if left-behind suit of evening clothes, turned out immaculately and with dignified ceremony by Yelping, still smarting from the offensive idea that his master could possibly stray farther than Bond Street without his genius valet (an idea that must have been beginning to occur to Mr. Fallon himself, somewhere on his way north with his mistress and his fiancée, no doubt an interesting situation best left undescribed in these pages), made his appearance at the step of his great-aunt's Queen Anne mansion in Upper Mount Street, it was indeed borne home to him that his lady-wife had become quite fashionable.

How else to account for the throng of famous faces illuminated by the flambeaux held upon the step by wigged and liveried footmen as they strolled from their own imposing dwellings, or dismounted upon the red carpet laid up to the front door from their elegant carriages. Jewels and silk glimmered in the light, and Peter was hailed with considerable more warmth than he had known in his bachelor days by such imperious doyennes of the upper ten thousand as Ladies Sefton, Jersey, and Castlereagh, each accompanied by their equally august spouses. His abil-

ity to make an appearance in town was lauded,
and he was stunned and amused to hear his wife
praised as a beauty, a grace, and an original who
kept them all entertained and enthralled. Without her, he was informed, it would have been a
Season of dull little debs and sad crushes of the
same old faces. Any gathering she graced with
her presence, he was informed by the lofty Mrs.
Drummond Burrell, instantly became a magical
event. Her flare, her style, her panache as a young
matron had lifted them all quite upward.

With these paeans ringing in his ears, Peter
was swept by the glittering throng into the house,
where Duddle, looking him up and down as he
relieved him of Gervais' walking stick and cha-
peau bas, informed him he was a real tulip.

Resisting the urge to disarray Duddle's best
wig, Lord Marchman merely inquired, "And
where is my wife?"

Duddle's eyebrows went up. "Why, at the top
of the stairs receiving, with her ladyship, my
lord," he answered. "Where else should she be
when this is her ball? Ah, Lady Ombersley! You're
in bloom tonight? Long win on the tables?"

Duddle was the same things to all men, Lord
Marchman reflected, trudging up the stairs behind the rustling silk trains of the ladies.

On the landing, Aunt Aurelia, resplendent in
towering ostrich plumes of a particularly eye-
popping shade of scarlet pinned with her famous
Star of Kurdistan to a turban of cloth-of-gold, a
figured shawl of spiderweb silk draped over her
plump arms, and every diamond she owned
pinned about the bodice of her scarlet and gold
figured silk gown, tapped her diamond-studded
ebony cane impatiently on the carpet and delivered him a particularly hawklike, self-satisfied

stare from her beady little eyes. This was how he could tell that she was pleased with him. "Ah," she said, extending two gloved fingers to him, nodding in approval at Gervais' finery. "I wonder if one shall forgive Gervais for running off to Gretna with Annabella and quite upsetting the seating arrangements at my table?"

Since in Peter's experience, such a remark meant that his great-aunt was enough in charity with the person thus addressed to consider making one of the numerous alterations of her will in their favor, he grinned roguishly. "I feel like a man-milliner in these togs, Aunt," he said frankly.

"Well, Peter, you look splendidly. After all, it is only once, and then you may go back to being as naval or as rural as you please. Now go and greet your wife." She waved him on with her cane, embracing one of her most despised contemporaries with a great display of affection.

It was only then that Peter noticed that the female standing beside his great-aunt was his wife, and he paused for a second, as if inhaling her very essence.

Sally had come from Hurlock's hands with that abigail exclaiming that she had not turned out one of her ladies so finely since Lady Aurelia's wedding, those many years ago. Her strawberry hair was brushed so that it gleamed beneath the candlelight, falling in soft tendrils about her face, pinned to the crown of her head with a mother-of-pearl cupid's knot. Pearl and diamonds droplets were suspended from her ears, and about her throat she wore the pearl and diamond collar that had been her parents' wedding present to her. A delicate flush was in her cheeks, and her eyes sparkled with animation as she allowed a rather gallant-looking gentleman to scribble his name into her dance program. She wore a gown of pale aquamarine, décolleté, and capped sleeves netted with silver spiderweb gauze figured with tiny flowers and birds and knotted with twisted bunches of cyclamen and aquamarine thread. The silver spiderweb overskirt opened to reveal the aquamarine silk skirt beneath, and the deep band of the hem repeated the design of silver spiderwebs and bands of cyclamen and aquamarine caught with the same threaded corsages. Upon her feet she wore ivory and silver striped slippers, and she carried an ivory fan, but no flowers.

Reluctantly, the gallant parted himself from her, and she turned, her smile wavering only a little as she beheld Peter.

Slowly, her eyes traveled up and down his finery, and he turned a finger beneath his collar, self-conscious. As lovely as she looked, he could not help but be aware that he rather yearned for his own Sally back in her riding habit or a plain muslin morning dress. Nonetheless, he took the hand she offered him, bending deeply over it.

"You do look beautifully fashionable, Sally," he said honestly.

"And you are quite handsomely elegant," she replied. "Peter." Somehow she wanted to laugh at both of them, and knew it would never do. Whatever had Peter put in his hair, to make it so oily and curled?

"May I have the honor of a dance with my own wife tonight?" he asked, almost shy.

Sally held out her program. She did not tell him that she had saved a waltz expressly for him, against many rivals, but he frowned nonetheless, at how many names he saw scrawled across the lines. Fashionable names. Elegant names.

"Listen, Sally, I—" he began in an undertone as he scribbled his name.

"Onward, Peter. People are waiting," the dowager said, prodding him with her cane.

Dinner, in the full elegance of Aunt Aurelia's dining room, surveyed by Duddle, was a ten-course affair for thirty couples. All of it, Peter noted without relish, thoroughly and fashionably badly cooked and tasteless, and served with a great many equally bad wines, of which he was careful to take only a sip or two, watching jealously as Sally laughed and chatted with ease to the handsome gentleman on either side of herself. Placed between a stone-deaf dowager who devoted her entire attention to an overdone mutton, and a vacuous and also chinless deb whose entire conversation seemed to consist of a waterfall of giggles whenever he addressed her, he was given a great deal of time to contemplate Sally's laughter, the way her brows drew together when she had a serious point to make.

When the ladies were excused from the table and the covers removed for port and cigarillos, he sat chafing in his seat, totally uninterested in the fate of Napoleon, Harriette Wilson, or Princess Charlotte and Prince Leopold. The Corn Laws bored him; they could repeal the statutes against murder for all that he cared, and he breathed a sullen sigh of relief when it was finally suggested that they join the ladies.

He would have sought the billiards room or the card tables until such time as his dance with his wife was called, but Aunt Aurelia was having none of it, and with a distinct flickering in her little hawklike eyes, he was presented to wallflower and antidote, spinster cousin and vapid

deb, for dance after dance until he thought he
would scream with frustration.

Aurelia had gone counter to the Season's fashion of ballrooms done up in pink silk tents and
bowers of roses, and instead had gone after what
Gervais had no doubt left as his legacy, a jungle
effect of hothouse plants and exotic flowers that
quickly wilted, along with Peter's shirt points,
in the heat.

Sally, on the contrary, seemed to be enjoying
herself immensely. At no time could it be said
that she flirted, or in any way conducted herself
unbecoming a young matron, but the mere sight
of his wife having a stunning time with a variety
of gentlemen richer, more fashionable, and more
handsome than himself was enough to set his
teeth on edge as yet another bovine female trod
upon his already aching toes, squeezed into Gervais' shoes.

When at last they called for the third waltz, he
was almost rude in the manner in which he de-
posited his partner upon her mama and strode
purposely across the floor toward his wife, surrounded by a claque of admirers, male and female.

"My dance, I believe," he said shortly, all but
dragging Sally out into the floor.

The strains of a soft waltz filled the room, the
sound of flowers floating upon a gentle stream.

Evidently, it was a tune Sally knew well, for
she hummed a little as they touched, moving
easily together, looking up into his eyes with just
a hint of a smile. "So, my lord," she said softly,
then giggled, "I cannot help but think about
Annabella and Gervais *et la belle Yvonne*—"

Peter laughed. "And very soon, if I have the
least idea, they will be joined by Aunt Theresa
and her nostrums and quackeries. I informed her

that I expected her to remove herself to Bath when I returned from London, but I imagine the prospect of free lodging with Gervais will suit her far better."

Sally's eyes grew very wide. "You did not! Oh, Peter! To cast her out!"

"Better her than my wife," Peter exclaimed. "Oh, Sally, what a bloody fool I've been, my love! To foist that pack of relations off upon you in that way."

"I am quite fond of Aunt Aurelia, you know, and of Gervais, also, although I think it was quite improper of him to set everyone talking by eloping with Annabella. They should be gossiping of us, you know!"

Peter nodded, grinning. "Yes, but only think of the lovely Yvonne! How tongues would wag then!"

Sally nodded. "London does seem to thrive on gossip. Peter?"

"Yes, my love?"

"I am the slightest bit tired of being fashionable. I am very, very grateful to Lady Aurelia, of course, and you will be furious when you see the bills, but"—she bit her lip, looking up at him—"I think I should very much like to come home."

"To America?"

"To Marchman Place, please. A month or two of this is all very well, once a year, Peter, but—"

"I hate it. I have always hated it. You silly goose, how would any female with as much common sense as you think that you weren't good enough for London? For England? You're worth all of them put together. It was my terrible family, wasn't it? Well, we shall have no more of relations."

Sally flushed slightly, looking away. "Well, I

am afraid we shall have some relatives, Peter. The colonel and Miss Henrietta are coming to visit. And someone else. A *mutual* relation."

"The colonel and Miss Henrietta?" Peter asked, slightly taken aback. Well, he supposed he could handle that. "And who else?" he demanded. "What mutual relation?"

The light, slowly dawning, left Peter dead in his tracks, staring at his wife. "Oh, dearest Sally, how long have you known?" he demanded, holding her very tightly.

She flushed prettily. "Well, I first suspected aboard ship, but thought it was seasickness, and then, when we came to Marchman Place, I wasn't certain I wanted to stay here—or have my child growing up in such an atmosphere!" She took on a mulish look.

"And now?" Peter asked.

"And now I am quite sure. Oh, don't look at me that way, its months and months away yet, but that is why the colonel and Miss Henrietta are coming. I am sure Mama will try to rule the nursery and Father will tell you how to improve your estates, but I suppose one of my brothers or another will marry soon, or Susannah will start to increase again, and then we shall deem them off."

"Or send them to Aunt Aurelia. She may make them as fashionable as she pleases. I'm sure that they may enjoy it for all of me. Oh, my dearest love, a baby!"

Fashionable London had never before been treated to the scandalous sight of a man kissing his own wife in the middle of the dance floor. It was hoped it was a scandal not to be repeated.

About the Author

Caroline Brooks is a practicing gerentologist who resides in Rising Sun, Maryland, with her husband and three children. Her interest in the Regency period was sparked when she purchased an old diary from that era in a Charing Cross bookstall during a visit to London in her student days.

SIGNET Regency Romances You'll Want to Read

Other Regency Romances You'll Enjoy